It Could HAPPEN...

A Family Adventure

J. Castillo

ISBN 978-1-63630-415-1 (Paperback)
ISBN 978-1-63630-416-8 (Digital)

Covenant Books, Inc.
11661 Hwy 707
Murrells Inlet, SC 29576
www.covenantbooks.com

This book I dedicate to my family, for without them, none of this would be possible. Understand that with my family, there is never a dull moment. The names of my family are their actual names. All other names are strictly coincidental. I based the book on a theory I have always thought about. Whether it is believable or not, this is purely fictional and not intended to replace what we know as our actual reality. Or is it?

CONTENTS

CHAPTER 1

THE CLAN

O f all the things unexplainable in this world we live in, there is a constant battle between two forces always—whether it is religion vs. science, data vs. hearsay, logic vs. illogic, perception vs. deception, political vs. nonpolitical, and so forth and so on. People are always trying to have an answer at all costs, and their answers favor their beliefs. Music is one field in which everyone has an opinion and is unwilling to accept anybody else's. Such groups argue or shall we say hotly debate on what the artist's intention was, without even thinking the artist might not have had any actual intention, only that the song sounded good to their ear and they recorded it.

Authors are also victims of these debates. Groups often debate about what an author was trying to say but wrote something else. So are all authors good at writing in parables such as in the Bible? To listen to these groups or individuals, one would think they wrote the song or book. Add all these dimensions to a work of art, whether they are right or wrong, whether accepted or declined, depending on what group you belong to—and there is an infinite number of them.

At work or in every occupation, there is at least one of these people:

First is the "Oh yeah, yeah" person. This person will ask a question; and as you answer it, out of the kindness of your heart, as you get to the end of the answer, they strike at you with their famous "Oh yeah, yeah" and then ignore you and walk off. Later in the day, you will find them telling someone, especially their boss, how miraculously they answered their question and saved the day.

Second is the "are you sure" person. This person is so insecure that by the time you finish with them, you are damn close to being afraid of the dark! You might be lucky to find your way home after this conversation, and you might remember the names of some of your family members. This conversation goes something like this: first the question and then a puzzled look on their face when you attempt to answer. The magic words follow, "Are you sure? Because I googled it and your answer is different." Now, a few seconds before you were confident in yourself and nothing could shake you, or at least you thought so. Your house of confidence has just gone from rock solid to melting jelly, and you do not understand how you got there. If you say "I'm sorry" for any minor thing, you have just had a large dose of insecurity from this "Are you sure?" person.

Third—and there are so many versions of this—is the "I thought you were smart!" person. That conversation goes something like this:

At one in the morning, I received a call from a coworker who was working the night shift. Part of the job was filling out a spreadsheet as to the night's activities.

"Hey, sorry to wake you up, but I need some help on the paperwork. Do you know what I need to put on the square on this spreadsheet?"

"Which square are you talking about?"

"The square on this spreadsheet."

"Where is the square, Joey?"

"On the spreadsheet."

"Okay, where on the spreadsheet?"

"Wow! It seems like you do not know! I will call someone that knows. Thanks."

So now you are wide awake, feeling like a real dumbass, because you did not know what to put on the square, thanks to Joey.

With all these opinions and dimensions added to almost any subject, it is a wonder we ever learn anything. In so many ways, we can project things. It just makes our world so much more complicated, or another version would be it makes our world more interesting—a prime example of how we have made everything in our world debatable.

We should always wonder when and where it started. Did it start with Lucy, the entire world's mom? One can only imagine if she started it. Was it something like "I don't like the brown grass because it makes me break out in hives. So I will eat the green one; it looks healthier"? The next morning it may have been "Oh no! Now I have to walk around with a green tongue. I will eat the gold one instead. Now I have a severe case of gas" and so forth and so on.

Wherever it began, it developed to a vicious level. Men compete and debate about trucks, guns, fishing, sports players, and even lawn mowing. No matter what you have or do, the other guy does it better and has something better than yours. And it is all a matter of opinion! Some men think of themselves as gourmet cooks, especially if they are from Louisiana. Being from there somehow gives them a birthright to be cooks, but very few of them work in any restaurant setting. Nowhere else is this more prevalent than in the oilfield of the USA. So if anybody is interested in going to work offshore on the rigs, don't bother; there are two guys in west Texas who have sucked all the oil out, and they did this while sitting in a trailer about one thousand miles away!

Women compete and debate on a different level. They stare at another woman when she walks into a place. They more than likely are competing on how they look. Women are far more vicious when competing, and we all know that. As opposed to men who are always lying, women are looking at details.

So, despite all this competing and debating, kids love their parents and are watching this and learning it; and it gets more vicious with every generation.

Keeping all the competition and debating in mind, our story begins with a family of six—Dad, Mom, daughter, son, middle son, and youngest son.

Dad enjoyed his children to where they ended up spoiled. He came from a family of ten, of which he was the youngest. Juan was the guinea pig for everything his brothers invented, such as rolling inside an old tractor tire, downhill! Now being the youngest member of his family, some of his brothers and sisters claimed spoiling him, an accusation they had yet to prove. Juan's life was uneventful—the usual school grind for twelve long years. After high school graduation, he went to a college in Monterrey, Mexico. Man! Was that culture shock! Since he grew up in South Texas, right on the border next to the Rio Grande. When he realized that was not for him, he joined the Army. Upon his return, he heard so many theories on what he should do that he just shut everyone off and went to work in the oilfield. He had an excellent job and supported his family and was happy doing it. At home, his pet peeve was keeping their yard in top shape. Minor repairs were no problem. Life had been good to him; and yes, there were trials, but the entire family got through them. Now all his life Juan thought he was of Mexican descent. He spoke good Tex-Mex Spanish, a border version of Spanish which mixes English and Spanish, and loved border cooking. He enjoyed taking family trips to the great southwest (Big Bend, New Mexico, Arizona). He did not feel comfortable in enormous cities with many people. Every time he visited the southwest, deep inside his head, he felt a calling of some sort and did not know why. His wife really enjoyed a few websites dealing with a person's ancestry. One day she convinced him to take a DNA test just to find out where he came from. Someone on that website contacted, and lo and behold! He had all the family trees! Juan came from a lengthy line of Chiricahua Apache! *How is that for a different dimension?* he thought. At last all that calling he had felt made sense, and it was not open for debate. He felt a lot of closure in his life now, and he was proud of his heritage now.

The matriarch of this small clan was the mom, Yolanda. She was the genius in the family. In contrast to Juan, she was the oldest in her family, which had three boys and two girls. Yolanda also grew up in south Texas and had the same qualities unique to the border—being well versed in Spanglish, border cooking, strong family ties, and highly intelligent. She grew up the same way as her husband; both he and her parents were of lower income, but life was great. She attended schools in south Texas, which were predominantly Hispanic, and this area even had their own accent. Yolanda got accepted to a college in south Texas and started her career in nursing. In direct contrast to her husband, Juan, she stuck to her guns and got an associate degree in nursing and started her medical career in a local hospital. Yolanda worked tirelessly for several years, becoming one of the best nurses in that hospital. Soon she got transferred to the medical intensive care unit, where only the nurses with excellent skills were. After a few more years, she went to work for a home health agency, where again she excelled and got assigned to a managerial position. Life was wonderful. She later went back to a four-year school and got a bachelor's degree in the nursing field. It was then that she opened her own home health agency. Things started going good now. Juan quit his job in the oilfield and went to work for her. As Juan later related, "Those were some of the best times in my life." Yolanda was the "glue" that held the clan together, with her wisdom, intelligence, and fairness. She also had this trait that very few people have, the gift of not imposing. It was something that had to be seen to explain it. She used that trait constantly, and it worked on everybody. There was no escape. She was also an outstanding cook. Some of her family was in Mexico, and it was from them she inherited her cooking gene. Her maternal grandmother was her hero from when she was at a young age. She was also the financial whiz of the clan. She could tangle with some of the best accountants. Yolanda was also good at reacting in emergency situations at home, when her husband was away at work. She could handle any situation without hesitation. She was the queen of rationale.

Then came the daughter, Alyssa, the big sister. She was the model type, always dressing and doing her makeup like a model. She was a tall slender woman, and she was always complaining about her weight. Now Alyssa was no slouch either. She was highly intelligent in her own way. She seemed to struggle more with common sense than books. She also went to the same college that her mother did, and again unlike her dad, she stuck to it and graduated with a career waiting for her in the medical field. Alyssa started her career as a PTA (physical therapist assistant) in south Texas. So now the clan had medical help on two sides. Now Alyssa had a unique talent. She could take any issue or situation and offer at least two versions of why the table was round, square, or brown. Once there appeared a pandemic in China, clear across the world, and she started preparing for it by stocking food and other household items. For the rest of the family, it was a world away, so it seemed like it was not especially important. Lo and behold, that pandemic shut down the world in the next few weeks. Also, during that pandemic, Alyssa showed the family a talent that no one knew about. Now during this pandemic, people in a state of panic had bought and cleaned out most stores of household items. Now the local news announced that everyone had to wear a mask when leaving their house. Well, the masks were all sold and there were no more available. This was when Alyssa showed one of her sides that no one knew existed. She made masks for the entire family, and these were better than the ones in some stores. People at stores would ask where they bought the masks. So they settled it that from that day forth, Alyssa would be the family seamstress and official mask maker. Alyssa was also quick to jump into action, albeit not always the right action. Attitude being 99 percent of an action, she had 110 percent, and that was enough.

Next came the oldest brother, Zeke. Even though he was far behind in years to Alyssa, he was turning into a hell of a fine adolescent man. Zeke was a respectful youthful man for the better part of the time, except he had a few downfalls here and there like any human being. Zeke was tenacious at carrying out a goal if he wanted it. His bigger interests were science and video games, which he turned out to be exceptionally good at. Another enormous interest for Zeke were cars. He could name the model, engine size, horsepower, and torque for any vehicle you can think of. He knew precise data of any engine and always liked the fastest cars in the world. Zeke had a hidden talent that his parents did not know existed. He was an exceptional tennis player. Nobody could figure out where this enormous interest came from. It was common knowledge that he was born with it and it was a gift from God. Zeke had competed in tournaments all over the state and could hold his own in any competition. All his teachers spoke very highly of him. Occasionally, in frustration, Zeke would have a meltdown, but would recuperate rather quickly. A soft-spoken child by nature, he fit in anywhere. Zeke was the child who could brighten anybody's day. His mother was always saying how kind-hearted and considerate Zeke was. When he was a baby, his normal eating hour was 8:00 p.m. To this day, he still would eat at 8:00 p.m. To show Zeke's tenacity, once after the family had moved from one city to another, the neighbor's kid was outside riding his bicycle. While Zeke's mother was talking to the kid's mom, Zeke was watching his every move. Now Zeke could still not ride a bike on his own. His bike still had training wheels, so he went to his dad and asked him to remove them.

His dad said, "You don't know how to ride without them."

Zeke said, "I am going to."

So his dad removed the training wheels; and on his third try, he could balance and ride it, still having trouble on the turns. He kept at it for several days, and on the third day, he was riding it without falling. His dad was so proud of him that he bought him a new bike. The next thing was roller skating. His parents took him to a skating rink, and when he saw kids roller skating, he had to learn it. He did.

So along came EJ, the middle son, rough and tough with "What you gonna do about it?" attitude. He was the rough dude of the family. He loved to headbutt you at a young age, but he had his tender moments with his family. He could be the sweetest child until something pissed him off. Every movie he ever watched, he would act it out in front of the family. So it was clear to all that he might end up in the movie business. He also liked toy cars, but not like his brother Zeke did. His parents stopped at a kids' zoo one day while traveling thru the southwest, and this petting zoo had a bunch of baby goats. Dad was carrying EJ because he wanted nothing to do with the goats. Dad tried to change his mind and set him down close to one of the baby goats. *Pow!* EJ swung at the goat, and luckily, he missed as that punch headed straight for the goat. No harm done. EJ would be the family's rough sports athlete, since we have to associate our children with some lifestyle when they are developing their character. Now EJ followed a lot of his big brother's habits, although on the rougher side. We have compared him to a certain cartoon character that goes around beating everything with a wooden club. He would bypass a meal for a bag of chips or candy, which is a trait most kids have at a young age. However, EJ sometimes wanted to be alone. He would go to the kids' playroom and just chill and watch a movie by himself and eventually fall asleep.

In walked the youngest family member, Emanuel Matias, alias "Manny." Manny was the "sly like a fox" member of the family. He had an uncanny ability to take something from you without you even knowing that he had. He was slick from a young age. When he was a toddler, he could swipe anything from under your nose, because he just had to taste it. No matter what the object was, "Someone has to verify the taste" was his motto. He got a hold of some hot chips that his older brother Zeke was eating, and he did not even skip a beat. He went for another one instantly. Manny even walked so lightly that you could not hear him until he was next to you. A lot of times he scared someone in the family, because the next thing they knew, he was standing next to them. Manny was also the determined one in the family. If he wanted something, he would not give up until he had it. Manny was a year younger than EJ, so there was a lot of competition for dominance, which is a natural human trait. His eyesight was as close to perfect as you can get since he could spot an insignificant speck of anything on the floor and taste it.

That completed the entire clan, as their dad called them. Both Mom and Dad were proud of their kids and all their accomplishments.

CHAPTER 2

THE ADVENTURE BEGINS

As we have seen in the prior chapter, this family is not unlike any other family in this world, each member having unique characteristics and abilities different from the other family members. Once they all come together, they form one bond, which makes them an extraordinarily powerful unit, each complementing the other. Other people being human will have their own opinion on how and why this happens.

So on we go.

Dad came home after two weeks of working away from the family, which was customary for him; so he was ready to spend some family time, and what better way than a road trip with the family.

"We are all going to go on a trip to the southwest." He was trying to go back in history and walk in the same footsteps of his ancestors.

There were two frowns. Mom said, "There is nothing out there. Very poor internet, TV coverage sucks, and a lot of nothing on the roads."

Zeke agreed to the trip right away because he enjoyed going through New Mexico, for whatever reason. "Are we going to go through New Mexico?" he asked in a joyous voice.

Aly asked, in a low tone, "What is it with you about New Mexico?"

"Maybe because I have never been to New Mexico," Zeke said.

Dad intervened, "Yes, you have son. You were just too young to remember."

Mom, being the rational person here, suggested a vote. "I think we should take a vote on whether we go west or east to big cities and *shopping!*"

Aly's eyes almost popped out of the sockets as she said, "I am with Mom on this one."

So on to the vote they went.

"Okay, who wants to go west, where the air is clean, there is no traffic, and we can breathe?" Dad asked.

Zeke raised his hand. "I want to go to New Mexico."

Meanwhile, EJ was just looking at everyone and listening to the conversation. Manny was standing next to him being noticeably quiet, a dead giveaway that he was up to something.

"I'll go west as long as I don't have to touch any animals," EJ commented.

So the vote was now three to two for going west. Dad, Zeke, and EJ were already making plans, when Mom jumped in and said, "Wait a minute! Manny hasn't voted."

Everyone turned to look at Manny, and he had a mouthful of candy. EJ and Manny had each gotten a fruit snack. Manny had eaten his, and during the voting conversation, EJ had dropped his guard and *wala!* Manny struck.

"Manny, we need to hear your vote," Mom said.

Manny just gave her a blank stare for a minute and then said, "Can I have more candy?"

"No, sir!" was the resounding answer from Mom and Aly at the same time as if they had rehearsed this.

So Manny resorted to his now famous blank stare and after a few seconds asked, "Can EJ have some more candy?"

When EJ heard this, he automatically started looking for his candy, and there was none.

He looked at Manny and asked, "Did you take my candy?"

"I thought you didn't want it," answered Manny, knowing it was too late for EJ.

"I was listening to Mom and Dad, you *dork!*" fired EJ.

16

"Manny, you need to stop taking other peoples' things," said Dad.

"It seemed like he didn't want them," answered Manny.

"It doesn't matter what it seems. The candies did not belong to you, and you don't decide that," Mom said.

Dad was more interested in the vote, so he asked, "Okay, Manny, what are you going to vote for?"

"I want to go west," said Manny, since EJ was giving him the evil eye.

And so the plan was to go west since Mom and Aly had lost the vote.

Dad and Mom started planning the trip to the great southwest. They planned a two-week excursion with some stops at places of interest. The first stop would be at Big Bend National Park for two days. Then they would head farther west into New Mexico, Land of Enchantment. In New Mexico, they planned to visit a reservation in San Carlos. The plan was to get hotel rooms as they got tired.

Aly got a friend to look after her dog, Thor, and serve as somebody coming to watch the house while they were gone. Dad took the family car to get it serviced, and everyone got excited about the trip. Mom baked some goodies to take along for the ride. Aly was busy planning her wardrobe. Zeke was online checking out how far the drive would be and checking out New Mexico, to make sure there were no Asian killer hornets there. Zeke was paranoid about flying insects, especially hornets. He just did not like insects, so he was always looking up information on them.

EJ was hiding somewhere in the house, just trying to be away from everybody. This was EJ's way of relaxing. He enjoyed playing alone. This way no one would try to borrow his toys. Mom got EJ's bag packed and asked EJ what small toys he wanted to take along.

"I'll just take my iPad," said EJ. So EJ packed his bag, and he was ready to go.

Mom had to ask Zeke to pack his bag. Zeke packed his clothes and was told by Mom to pack some pants also, because she knew that Zeke was a perpetual shorts wearer. He would wear nothing else. Even in winter he would try to wear shorts.

Manny had no preference; he was too interested in taking something and not getting caught. Manny was more interested in the goodies that Mom would pack for the trip. He loved bread and hoped that would be in the bag. He was ready to go when everybody was.

Meanwhile, Aly was always seeking Mom's advice on what to pack. It was the usual designer everything and a lot of makeup stuff. Dad still had not returned, so Mom started packing her bags. Mom and Aly were not very fond of going west, since all the best shopping was on the east; but they wanted to keep everybody happy, so they acted excited.

Finally, Dad came in from getting the family car ready. "We leave tomorrow at 7:00 a.m. Everyone, get a good night's sleep and be ready to ship out tomorrow."

CHAPTER 3

THE UNEXPECTED

The next morning was hectic, as everyone was trying to get ready, and the house was just full of hustle and bustle. Everyone was asking questions and trying to remember what they were taking along on the trip. Dad was getting the car ready to pack. The kids were all trying to get to the bathroom, and all were being used. Mom was in one getting ready. Aly was in the other one, also getting ready.

Dad came in the house. "The car is ready to load, for whoever is ready," he said.

"You can start with the kids' stuff, please," Mom said.

So Dad started getting Zeke's, EJ's, and Manny's stuff to put it in the car. The excited kids asked if they could play outside, while everybody else got ready. Dad told them if they would not get all dirty, it was okay.

Mom overrode that quickly, "No! You don't. You'll stay in here until everyone is ready!"

Dad just looked at the boys and shrugged his shoulders.

Finally, everyone was ready, and the car got packed.

"Zeke, did you bring the walkie-talkies?" Dad asked.

"I'll get them, Dad," Zeke answered.

So EJ and Manny got in the car and took their assigned places. Aly got in the car and took her place. Zeke got in and handed Dad the walkie-talkies.

Mom sat in the front seat, and Dad checked the house and made sure they had locked everything. Dad liked to leave the TV on, because he said that way people would think there was somebody home. Dad got in the car and started it, and off they went on their road trip.

Manny was the first to fall asleep after they had gone about seventy-five miles. Then EJ dozed off until there was a call for a pit stop from Zeke way in the back of the car. Dad looked for a secluded stop, and then Zeke did his thing. Manny woke up again, EJ regained his alertness, and everyone talked after a long moment of silence. Mom and Dad started discussing the accommodations at Big Bend National Park for that night. She had rented a cabin out in the woods for two nights. Dad agreed that it would be a nice place to stay, and the kids could learn a lot about nature. Mom acted like she liked the idea, but Dad knew that Mom and Aly's idea of camping was at the Gardens of the Hyatt Regency Hotel. As they traveled along the highway, Dad gave the kids a guided tour of the area and explained to them they would sleep close to the clouds tonight. EJ and Manny could not understand what he meant.

So Zeke sprang into action. "Dad means we will drive up some gigantic mountains. The cabin where we will sleep is up on those mountains. I am the expert because Mom and Dad brought me here when I was your age. So I'll give you two munchkins permission to call me Mr. Expert."

Now it was common knowledge that the road to Big Bend was long and lonely, so Dad let the conversation go on. Finally, after a while Manny went back to sleep, and EJ got drowsy again and fell asleep. Zeke fell asleep in the time somewhere between Manny and EJ. Aly was next. As Dad looked in the mirror, everyone was asleep in the back. Mom had been reading a book, and now she too was in La La Land. Dad pushed on and kept driving to keep their schedule on track. While everyone was asleep, a big-horned owl flew just over the car; and Dad did not know whether he was getting tired or what, because he could have sworn that the owl had a human face. Dad blinked his eyes hard and then started thinking about what could have made him see that. So Dad tried to make sense of what his eyes had just seen. He thought, *Well, it all happened so fast. Maybe it was just the angle, or reflection, as the owl flew by. There is no way. I know it has a suitable explanation.*

Dad was now looking at any bird close to the highway, but they all looked normal. So he kept pressing on to keep on schedule, but the image of that bird kept coming back. He kept saying to himself, *I know I imagined that. Had to be the angle of the sunlight or something like that.*

After two hours Mom woke up, and now Dad had someone to talk to.

"How much longer to Big Bend?" Mom asked.

"About another hour and a half or so," Dad answered. Then everybody woke up when they heard Mom and Dad talking. Then came the famous road trip question, "Are we there yet?"

"Almost," Dad answered.

Mom asked if anybody was ready for some goodies she had packed. Manny was the first one to say yes. EJ was still groggy, so he did not answer. Zeke was a resounding "*Yes!*" Mom had baked some cookies and made chicken salad sandwiches and chips, and Coke was also in the ice chest. Dad stopped the car and got everybody a Coke from the ice chest. Everyone was eating as the trip continued. The chatter was on while everyone was eating. Mom asked Dad if he was getting tired yet. Now Dad was used to driving longer distances because of his job. So he answered that he was not tired, but in the back of his mind was the image of that owl, and it was eating at him.

They finally made it to Big Bend. Aly and Mom wanted pictures of the family next to the big stone marker at the entrance of the park. Dad stopped and everyone took pictures, and Dad was excited, but was still trying to figure out in his mind the image of that bird.

Once they made it to the cabins' office, they discovered there was a restaurant there too. So they checked in, and everyone decided they wanted to eat at the restaurant. Everyone was planning to get to the small store also on that resort. When everyone was seated, the waiter came by to take the order.

Suddenly, Aly's face was pale, and she just pointed at her thigh. On her thigh was the biggest walking stick that the entire world had ever seen. Dad told her not to move, and she sat still. By this time, the waiter was back; and he took a napkin, put it over the walking stick, and carried it outside the restaurant. As he came back, he apologized to everyone and said that it happened sometimes with all kinds of animals. He related the story about the raccoon that once came in the restaurant in the wee hours of the morning and did not want to leave.

After everybody had their meal, they all headed to the cabin; and on everyone's mind was the question, *Are there bugs in the cabin?* When the lights came on in the cabin, Dad and Zeke inspected every crack and crevice and gave the all clear. Everyone felt relieved and tried to settle down for the next two days.

It was still daylight. So everyone sat on some lawn chairs that were available. Dad asked the boys if they wanted to walk around for a bit and explore. They all agreed and went off into the woods. Mom and Aly stayed outside the cabin and just relaxed. As they were walking back to the cabin, Dad noticed that Mom had gone inside and Aly was still sitting outside. Once they got there, the boys all ran inside, and Dad sat outside with Aly. He noticed that she looked nervous and asked if she was okay.

Aly turned to him and said, "I'm okay, Dad."

"Are you sure?" Dad asked. "You look very nervous."

"It's just the trip, all that time in the car," she said.

Dad knew her better than that, so he kept insisting, "Are you sure?"

Finally, Aly said, "You promise not to tell anyone?"

Dad said, "Scout's honor."

"Okay, I will tell you, but you promise."

Dad said, "Promise."

She started, "You know I wasn't really scared of the walking stick, because it's just an insect."

Dad said, "It's okay. I'm afraid of those too!"

"You didn't let me finish. When I first saw it on my leg, that thing had a human face!" She bowed her head, thinking she looked foolish to her dad.

"*Whoa*!" Dad said in a scared voice. Then he looked at Aly and said, "Do not feel bad, sweetheart. There are a lot of weird things out here."

"But a face on a walking stick!" exclaimed Aly. Somehow Dad knew exactly how she felt. Aly was really embarrassed after she revealed her story to Dad.

Dad turned to Aly and said, "I believe you."

Aly said, "What?!"

Dad said, "Now I need to tell someone about what I saw. I don't want to scare your mom, but I need to tell it."

Aly was all ears, not expecting what she would hear.

Dad started out, "As we were driving up here, everybody fell asleep. Then I saw this big-horned owl flying toward the car on the highway. When he flew over the car, I saw it had a human face on it! I was hoping it was my brain or vision playing tricks on me, and I have been trying to figure out what could have caused it—sunlight, windshield glare, or something. But now that I hear your story, I am not so sure." By now it was dark outside, and Dad suggested that everybody go inside and they discuss it in the morning.

Morning came and everyone woke up. Dad asked if everyone wanted to spend another day there or move on, hoping for the latter. Mom suggested they have some breakfast at the restaurant and decide there.

Everyone agreed, especially Manny.

Dad said, "Open the door slowly. I hear the javelinas gather outside the front doors of the cabins, waiting to get fed."

Mom said, "I will. I read that too. We have some sandwiches left over. When everybody is ready, I'll toss them out; and when they go for the sandwiches, we can get to the car."

Zeke said, "I want to throw the sandwiches to the javelinas."

Mom said, "Whew! I was hoping somebody would volunteer."

So Zeke had the sandwiches ready for when everybody was ready. They heard the javelinas snorting outside their front door.

Dad said, "Here, let me help you do that."

Zeke said, "I want to do it," so Dad agreed and he and Mom did it.

When everybody was in the car, Mom and Zeke looked like they had just seen a ghost.

Mom suggested, "Why don't we keep going out of here and eat breakfast further down the road?"

Everyone agreed, except Manny, but they outvoted him. So they drove to the next small town and had breakfast.

While they were eating, Zeke asked Mom, "What did you hear from those javelinas?"

Mom made a gesture to Zeke, like zip it!

Dad looked at Aly, and Aly was already looking at Dad.

"What do you mean, Zeke?" asked Dad.

"Oh, I just thought I heard something, but it would not be possible," said Zeke.

Dad looked at Mom and said, "You were there."

Mom just looked at Dad and told Zeke, "Tell him, Zeke."

"Okay, when we opened the door, the javelinas took off running. Then me and Mom heard one of them say, '*Run*. Get away from the viruses," and I thought I was the only one that heard it. And when I looked at Mom, I knew she had heard it too."

Dad admitted that it was the best thing getting away from that place, and Mom asked why. Dad looked at Aly and told her to tell them her story.

Aly said, "You remember the walking stick?" Everyone nodded. Then she said, "What scared me was that it had a human face!" You could have heard a pin drop, even Manny stopped eating.

Mom said, "Okay, Dad, what happened to you?"

Dad started, "On the way here, you all were asleep, and I saw this horned owl flying toward us on the highway. I slowed down hoping it would fly higher, so I wouldn't hit it. When he flew right over the car, he had a...a...human face! So I say let's get out of here and continue to where we are going."

Manny quickly jumped in and said, "Me and EJ saw something too!"

"What did you see?" asked Dad.

"Well, when me and EJ went to the restroom at the gas station we stopped by, there was a dog outside the restroom, and he kept sticking his tongue out at us," said Manny.

"Then what happened?" asked Mom.

"EJ kicked him in the nuts."

"EJ!" Mom said.

"Well, I warned him, Mom, and he kept doing it. I warned him twice, and he said *make me*," said EJ.

"He didn't bite you?" asked Dad.

Manny said, "No, he took off running, and he would stop and lick his balls and then keep on running."

CHAPTER 4

PUSHING ON

After they revealed all their stories, they took off again. The ride was long and quiet.

Suddenly Mom spoke and said, "Did we really go through that?"

Dad said, "I have been trying to figure it out in my head all this time, and I can't. Get some sleep. You look like you need it. I'll hold the fort."

Finally, they left Texas and drove into New Mexico. Dad woke Zeke up because he wanted to know when they crossed into New Mexico. When Zeke woke up, so did everyone else. Manny was hungry again. All the goodies were all gone, so Dad stopped to get him a Coke from the back of the car. When he got off the car, he noticed that there was a weird noise coming from the brush on the other side of the highway.

When he got in the car, he said, "There is a strange buzzing sound outside, probably the electricity going through the power lines."

As they took off again, they all heard the buzzing sound, and it went away instantly. Nobody worried about the noise since it went away quickly. Again, they drove off, and everybody was listening to Manny describe how the dog took off, and all were laughing.

Suddenly, there was this blinding flash of a dazzling light that blinded everybody. When it was over, Dad was in the road's ditch.

They were all scared and trying to regain their eyesight. Dad was the first one, and when he looked around, they were off the road; but the road had changed. It was no longer an interstate, and it looked like an old and battered road. Dad's first reaction was to get off and find out what was going on.

Mom stopped him. "Wait. Don't go out there yet. Let's see what's going on from in here; and, kids, lock your doors."

They waited for about half an hour, and nothing or no one was around them. Dad decided he would check it out.

He said, "As soon as I get out, lock the doors."

Mom worried because when she started looking around, the surroundings looked different from before the flash. Dad got out of the car, and there was an eerie quiet. He walked around the car and checked to see if there was any damage to the car. The car looked all right, and Dad went back in, and the car started right away.

After a conversation with everyone, they all voted to turn back, since all this was strange. So Dad made a U-turn, and they headed back home. After a while of driving on the torn-up road, they pulled over and checked things out. To their surprise, they were right back where they had started. Dad was confused, and he thought the place just looked familiar. So he crossed the road and was horrified to see their car tracks and the bottle Zeke had thrown out the window. Dad was really confused now. He looked at his watch, and it was already getting late.

He went back in the car and told everybody, "We need to find a place to stay."

Mom was worried, and she asked if they had gone in a circle or something to end up in the same place.

Dad said, "I don't know, but something is wrong here."

So they drove off again and after hours ended up in the same place and exceptionally low on gasoline, and there was nowhere to buy any. So Mom and Dad decided that the only thing to do was sleep there with their doors locked. Everybody was awake, and no one could fall asleep. Finally, way in the distance, they saw some headlights coming. As they came closer and closer, they seemed to slow down. Then they stopped across the road. Dad was watching them closely as the door opened. It was another man. He came over to their car and lightly tapped on the window.

"Can I help you?" Dad asked, as he just barely opened the window.

"Yes, please, we got lost and are going around in circles," the man said.

"There seems to be a lot of that going around," Dad answered.

"Are you lost too?" the man asked.

"Yes, we drive for a while and we end up in the same spot, only going the other way," answered Dad.

Just then they heard a voice say, "You have to drive around three times."

They both turned, trying to figure where the voice came from. All they could see was a black bird sitting on the fence wire. They kept looking and could see no one other than the bird.

Dad approached the bird and asked, "Did you just say something?"

The bird just looked at him, as any normal bird would. Now Dad had gotten close to it. Then it hit him. The bird didn't fly away!

He whispered to the other man, "Did you notice anything strange?"

"With the bird?" asked the man.

"Yes," said Dad.

"No, not really," said the man.

"We were two feet away from it, and it didn't fly away!" said Dad.

"You're right!" said the man.

As soon as they turned their back to it, the bird spoke again, "You two don't even realize how impolite it is to talk to someone when you are facing them?"

Dad and the man were more confused now.

So Dad, with his back toward the bird, asked him, "So we go around three times to the same place?"

"What are you, two geniuses or something?" said the bird.

"Geniuses?" Dad asked.

"Yes, a life form that is dumb, in case that was your next question," the bird said.

"Don't you mean a moron?" asked Dad.

"Look. If you were morons, you would not get lost; and besides, you are the first viruses that I see trying to get somewhere in one circle. I am out of here. You geniuses might be contagious, so later." And he flew away.

"Can you explain what just happened?" asked the man.

"Hell no!" answered Dad. "From what I saw, and I still do not believe it, it considered us impolite if we spoke to it while facing it. He also called us geniuses, which I think is opposite of moron, because when I asked if he meant moron, he said we would not get lost if we were morons; but the thing that bothered me was that he referred to us as viruses."

By now Mom and the kids were getting restless in the car, so they opened the windows to get fresh air. Dad walked over to where Mom was and explained to her what had just happened. By now the other man's wife had exited their car and walked over to where everyone was.

"Hello," she said to Mom and the kids.

"Hello," everyone answered.

"I am Ramona, and this is Leilani and Isabela," referring to her daughters, who were standing next to her.

"Hello," everyone answered from inside the car.

Mom introduced everyone, "This is Aly, Zeke, EJ, and Manny. At the moment, we are all terrified!" said Mom.

So Mom asked everyone if they wanted to get off the car. She got a resounding "Yes!"

The man came over to Dad and said, "I'm Ramon."

"Nice to meet you, Ramon. I'm Juan and this is my wife, Yolanda."

"Hello," said Ramon.

Dad told everyone what had just happened to him and Ramon and was thinking to himself, *How did we end up in this backward place?* So he told Ramon about when they left home, the owl, the walking stick, and the javelinas—also about the big flash they had been through.

Ramon said they had also experienced the same, but they had left a week before. How they had been in the same spot for who knows how long no one knew. Dad asked him if he had stopped at all and run into any strange things like the bird.

"I wanted to stop, but it really terrified Ramona and the girls," said Ramon. "One thing I noticed is that the more I drive, my gas gauge reads closer and closer to full, instead of going to empty."

Dad suggested that they go three times to the same place to see what would happen.

Everyone was afraid, but there wasn't much of a choice. Ramon decided they would follow them. Off they went on their third time around. When they got to the place they had been, the road led them straight now, and Dad noticed that the gas tank was full now. They drove for an hour. Then suddenly there appeared what seemed like a gas station with a store on the horizon. As they drove closer, they noticed it was a store. So Dad pulled into the parking lot, and Ramon followed.

Everyone was hungry and wanted snacks. Dad and Ramon went into the store.

As they approached the counter, a voice said, "That's far enough!"

Dad and Ramon stopped and asked. Then they remembered and faced away from the man sitting on a chair behind the counter.

"We are not from around here, and we would like to buy some snacks and Coke for our kids. Do you have any of that?"

"Sure do," said the man. "But you can't buy them today."

"Why?" asked Dad.

"Because it ain't your day today," said the man. "Today is anti-body day."

"Antibody day?" asked Dad.

"Yup," said the man.

"Can I ask what an antibody looks like?" asked Ramon.

That was when the man lifted his baseball cap, and to their enormous surprise, it was a *bear* wearing clothes!

"You're looking at one," said the man or bear. "Now you viruses may not buy today, till tomorrow," he continued.

"Why are we called viruses?" Dad asked.

Then the bear got aggravated. "Boy, don't you know anything? Did you go to college or something? They know you as viruses because you make Mr. Host sick."

Now, Dad had seen some houses behind the store as they drove up and asked the bear, "Does somebody live in those houses?"

"No, but if you want to rent them, I can only afford to pay 165 for each house," said the bear.

"You'll pay us to rent the houses?" asked Dad.

"Okay, two hundred each and not one million more. Take it or leave it. I'm sure someone will come along sooner."

"Can we see them?" asked Ramon. There was no answer.

Dad gave Ramon the signal to turn around and not face the bear.

"There, that's better," said the bear. "Your friend is smarter than you are. Don't you know it is impolite to talk to someone when you are facing them?"

"Sorry," said Ramon.

The bear agreed to show them the houses. As they were walking to them, Dad asked him if the houses were in good shape.

"No, they are dumps. Everything works in them, but what do you expect for two hundred dollars?"

When they went inside the first house, were they surprised. It was luxurious, with a lot of living space, and the kitchen was outstanding. So Dad and Ramon told the bear he had a deal. Dad and Ramon went back to the cars and brought Mom and Ramona to see the houses. Mom worried about not being able to go home. Dad worried but thought about staying here until they figured out how to get home. They talked to Ramon and Ramona, and they all agreed to stay until they figured how to get the heck out of here.

CHAPTER 5

AN ENTIRE NEW WORLD

As they moved into their house, Mom worried about furniture, and Aly worried about her bed and if she would have her own bathroom. Dad explained to them they had to see this. From the outside, it looked like a little shanty; but once inside, it became a mansion.

When they got inside, Mom looked around, and there was a big beautiful kitchen. Aly chose her room, and it had an enormous bathroom with a Jacuzzi in it. Zeke picked his room. It had a PlayStation, a humongous TV, and its own bathroom. EJ and Manny wanted to room together, and when they saw their room, they were excited. It had a huge TV and a twin bed—one was a fire engine and the other a race car. It had a giant closet packed with toys. Mom and Dad's room was enormous, with a king-size bed, a massager, heat, a cooler, a giant ceiling fan, and an even bigger TV. If they walked to the backyard from inside the house, it was huge and had a tennis court, swings, and a gigantic swimming pool. If they walked to the backyard from the outside of the house, there was nothing but dried weeds and thorns.

So, the next day, they all went to the store to buy food. The bear was there and was counting some boxes.

When everyone walked in, he said, "I was just gonna have our trash delivered to your house."

Mom quickly reacted, "Excuse me!"

"Well, your husband said he wanted to buy food, and you viruses eat trash, so I was gonna deliver it."

Dad intervened, "You got it all wrong, there, Mr. Bear! We want to buy food, not trash."

"This is good trash. Let me show you," said the bear.

As he opened one box, the smell of roast beef was exceptional. Other boxes had the most beautiful veggies Dad had ever seen. There was freshly baked bread, milk, and everything you could think of. Mom and Dad looked at each other and agreed, "Okay, we will take your version of trash. How much do we owe you?" asked Dad.

"You viruses are always trying to strike a deal!" said the bear. "I can't give you more than three hundred dollars for it. If not, I will make money, and I can't do that."

"Three hundred and twenty-five," said Dad.

"I can't turn down a good deal. Okay, it's yours," said the bear.

Mom and Dad seemed confused now.

Dad asked the bear, "What is your name?"

"AB3," said the bear.

"So what do we call you, so we won't be saying Mr. Bear?" asked Dad.

"AB3 is my name," said the bear.

"So can we call you AB?" asked Dad.

"No, my name is AB3," said the bear.

"Okay, AB3 it is," said Dad.

The bear paid Dad for taking the food or trash, and the family was on their way.

"This place is so stupid," Mom complained. "Nothing makes sense."

"Well, we have always lived in a place where right is right and left is left. Apparently here it is opposite of everything we have ever known. Everything is backward to us, but I wonder who Mr. Host is. The bear keeps mentioning him. He said we make Mr. Host sick?" said Dad.

"I wish we could leave this place now," Mom exclaimed. "It is getting on my nerves."

Suddenly there was a knock on the door. Dad answered it and saw Ramon standing there, and he was as pale as a ghost.

"Are you okay, Ramon?" asked Dad.

"No," answered Ramon, "our dog just showed up, and he talks; and he told us he has known about this other world for years, and that's when we realized that we could be here for a while, the way he explained it."

"Calm down, Ramon. We will find a way out of this eventually and go back to where we came from," explained Dad. "You just need to relax and think about it. At least we have our families with us, and together, we will find a way."

"I'm just thankful that my family is not the only humans, or what they refer to as viruses, and it's good to have you all here too. And yes, together we will find a way out of this. I'll go back to our place, and if you hear or think of anything for us to help, please let us know and we will do the same," said Ramon.

"We sure will, Ramon. I promise you," said Dad, trying to reassure Ramon.

Mom and Dad put the kids to bed and decided they would take turns standing watch for a few nights in case anything "weird" happened. Aly heard their conversation and offered to help. They would each pull an eight-hour watch, with Dad taking the night watch from 11:00 p.m. to 7:00 a.m. Mom would watch from 7:00 a.m. to 3:00 p.m. and Aly from 3:00 p.m. to 11:00 p.m.

The next morning came, and everything was quiet throughout the night. Dad slept for a few hours while Mom was on watch, then woke up, and helped with the kids. The boys didn't seem to worry about what was going on, except Zeke; but he tried not to show it, so Mom would not get more nervous.

"What do you think about this whole situation, Zeke?" Dad asked.

"Well, I don't like it, but at least we are all together, and we are not alone. Can you imagine if we were going through this alone?" commented Zeke.

Dad thought of everyone in the family. Zeke was calmer and realistic about the whole thing. Dad now asked Aly the same question.

"Well, I have to go with Zeke on this one, but I still wish we would have gone shopping, instead of coming out here," said Aly.

"*Amen!*" Mom said, angrily.

"What do you feel?" Dad asked Mom.

"Well, I am happy that we are all together, and I was kidding about the shopping. We had no way of knowing this was gonna happen to us, so I am glad that we have each other to count on," said Mom.

"That sure is nice to hear. I was feeling so guilty about bringing everyone out here. This was not my plan at all, but I promise you all that I will never stop looking for a way out of here," said Dad.

Then EJ and Manny walked in the room where the conversations were taking place.

Dad asked them, "I know you two are too young to understand what happened to us, but I need to include you. How do you feel about what happened to us?"

Manny thoughtfully answered, "Well, Dad, I love you, Mom, Aly, Zeke, and EJ; and I heard what Zeke said, and I like it. We are together and I am happy, but I am also happy about all the food we got and the big room we have, and I love my bed and my TV."

"How about you, EJ?" Dad asked.

EJ said, "I don't like all these animals around me, and if another dog sticks his tongue out at me..."

"Okay, okay," Dad intervened. "We get the picture."

Suddenly there was another knock on the door. Dad opened it; and to everyone's surprise, there was a goat in a uniform, standing there.

So Dad turned his back to him and asked, "Hello, can I help you?"

"I don't need any help, and why are you saying that? You still have to pay your utilities bill. Now it is $150. Sign here, and here is your bill," said the goat.

Dad looked confused when the goat handed him $150.

"From now on it will come in the mail. Hello and have an awful day," said the goat.

"What was that all about?" asked a confused Mom.

"I do not understand what just happened," answered Dad. "Apparently, everything being opposite, we get paid for using utilities. If you look at it, is that really a terrible thing?"

Mom just looked dazed and shook her head.

CHAPTER 6

ALY'S WORLD

This calm and warm morning, Mom remembered she had left her purse in the car and asked Aly if she would be kind enough to get it. Aly hurried to the door and went outside, and the air felt so nice to her after being in the house for so long. As she was trying to get Mom's purse, she heard a voice ask, "What are you looking for?"

It was a high-pitched voice, like that of a little girl. Aly turned and could see nobody, and this gave her goose bumps, and she was afraid because she had not faced these things by herself yet.

Finally, when she looked downward, on the other side of the car was a small white poodle, with ribbons on her ears. Aly remembered that she had to give the dog her back before saying anything.

"I am looking for my mom's purse," replied Aly.

"What's that, and what is a mom?" asked the poodle.

"Well, a purse is where women store the stuff they need to carry with them. A mom is the one that gives us birth," said Aly.

"Oh, okay, a purse is like a storage?" said the poodle.

"Yes," answered Aly.

The poodle then asked, "A mom is your carrier?" Aly looked confused. So the dog explained, "Look. A carrier is the one that carries you until you are born. Geez! You viruses are so intelligent!"

Aly wondered, *No wonder EJ kicked the other dog in the nuts! She smarts off again, and I'll do the same!*

37

"What is your name?" Aly asked.

The dog did not answer. Aly then remembered that she had to face away from it.

"What is your name?" she asked again.

"I am AB5, and who are you?" the dog asked.

"My name is Aly. Nice to meet you. Can we be friends?"

"Why do you want to be my friend? Don't you like me?" asked the dog.

"Yes, I like you," answered Aly.

"Then why do you want to be a friend? Only those that hate each other are friends," said the dog.

Now Aly got confused, but she remembered that everything in this place was backward.

"Okay, if I like you, then what are we?" asked Aly.

"We would be rivals, and if we get to be good rivals, then we would be bitter rivals. We call it BBR," the dog said as her eyes got bigger with excitement.

"Okay, we can be rivals," said Aly.

"I'll ask my carrier if it's okay to be rivals with a virus," said the dog. "I have to go now, but I'll be back," she said as she took off.

Aly just stood there and wondered if she was freaking out or what. The dog was a pretty dog, but somehow, she had a hard time believing that she had just had a conversation with a dog. She remembered her dog, Thor, back home and thought about how much she missed him. Was he getting fed? Was he okay all alone? A few tears came to her eyes as she kept wondering how he must feel, lonely and missing the family, except Dad. She sat down on a log which was lying next to the house. Then she remembered the walking stick and got up quickly and looked all around, hoping to not see any bugs. Then to her surprise, there was a hedgehog underneath the log.

He came out dusting himself off and said, "Who do you think you are, squashing me like that?"

Aly almost fainted, but she got herself together and held her composure. "I didn't know you were under there!" she said.

"Well, you need to ask next time!" said the hedgehog. He then started looking at her peculiarly and said, "Wait a minute! Don't I know you from somewhere?"

"Why would you know me?" Aly asked.

"Well, a long time ago, I lived in somewhere, and I remember someone like you," he said. "I was much younger, but I moved here from somewhere." Aly was now thoroughly confused and did not want to have this conversation. "You don't remember me, do you?" said the hedgehog.

"No, I don't," said Aly.

"You were very young back then," said the hedgehog.

So Aly sat back down and thought about it and lost track of time. She could not believe the conversations she was having with all these critters. She tried to think back to when she was a little girl. Then it hit her! She had a hedgehog pet at one time! Could it be that same hedgehog? All these things were crossing through her mind, and she dozed off and fell asleep.

Next thing she heard was a voice calling her name, "Aly! Aly!"

She woke up hoping all this had been a nightmare, but the same house was still there, with the log and the rock she fell asleep on. She did not want to answer, but as the voice got closer, she recognized Zeke's voice.

"Aly," said Zeke, "Mom wants you. She sent me to go looking for you, because they worried that you never came back inside."

Dad also came from the other direction, and EJ and Manny were with him. "Are you okay, Aly?" Dad asked. "Me, Mom, Zeke, EJ, and Manny were really worried about you."

"I'm okay," said Aly, "but boy, have I got something to tell you guys!"

Dad walked behind everyone to make sure all the kids went inside. Dad locked all the doors and made sure all the windows were closed. He still did not feel comfortable at all in this place.

The next morning Aly was still wondering if that was the same hedgehog. She went to the kitchen where Mom was cooking break-fast and sat down on one of the fancy stools they had.

Mom saw the look on her face and asked, "Are you okay, baby?"

Aly just shook her head and said, "Mom, something weird happened yesterday."

"What happened?" asked Mom.

Dad walked in and said, "Hold on, Aly. Let's wait for everybody to be here so we know what to look for in this weird place."

So Dad woke everybody up, and everybody had been nervous, so they got up quickly and all headed to the kitchen.

"Okay, go ahead, Aly," said Dad.

Aly said, "I hope nobody thinks I'm crazy!"

Dad said, "No one will, sweetheart. We are all scared and worried, so anything we learn about this place will help all of us."

"Okay, here goes. Yesterday when I went to get Mom's purse from the car, I heard like a little girl's voice, asking me what I was doing. I turned and didn't see anybody there, so I thought I had just imagined it. Then I went to the other side of the car, and there was a young poodle standing there. She wanted to know what I was doing. Then she wanted to know what a purse was and what a mom was. She told me that moms in this place are called carriers. So I was freaking out, so I sat on the log that's lying next to the house. Then I remembered the walking stick at the restaurant and quickly got up. This hedgehog came out from under the log, and he was mad because I had nearly crushed him. Then he said he knew me from somewhere, so I asked him from where, and he kept saying somewhere. He also said that when he knew me, I was a young child. That's when I went to the big rock and lay down on it. The next thing I heard was Zeke looking for me. I realized I had fallen asleep and woke up hoping the nightmare was over, but I wasn't that lucky. I also thought a lot about Thor, how he must be home alone and missing all of us. I can't even call to see if he is being fed or not. All of this made me cry, and I fell asleep. But I have never been happier than when I saw everybody and that I was not alone," said Aly.

"It's okay now, baby. You are safe in here with all of us," said Mom.

Dad backed up the statement. Dad said, "Later on today, we will all try to make sense of all this."

After breakfast, everyone got together and went outside by the log again. This time Aly felt a lot safer and braver because everyone was with her. Aly stood up on the log and jumped on it twice, and out flying came the hedgehog.

"Why do you keep bothering me like that?" the hedgehog asked.

"Because I want to know where you know me from!" said Aly in a demanding voice.

"I already told you when we were in somewhere," said the hedgehog.

"What do you mean by somewhere?" Dad asked.

"That's where you came from," said the hedgehog.

"I know we came from somewhere. Everybody did, but what do you mean?" Dad asked.

"Oh, I forgot viruses can't remember anything. Okay, somewhere refers to the place you came from. Your world is referred to as somewhere."

Aly said, "So how were you in our world and then in this one?"

"Okay, you got time?" asked the hedgehog.

"We got nothing but time," answered Dad.

The hedgehog took a seat on a slight rock and told all. "I was born in your world, or somewhere. When I was a baby hedgehog, some viruses like you trapped me. Then I got taken to what you guys call a pet store. In this pet store were a bunch of other antibodies that had gotten captured by viruses too. Now, the viruses did not know that we could understand what they were saying, but we understood every word, and it confused us how backward your world was. Being antibodies, we have taken an oath that if they capture us, we shall not reveal the extent of our knowledge. Our purpose in life is simple, to protect Mr. Host from any illness. So, after being in that pet store for a while, this little girl took me with her. You all call it buy. This little girl took me home with her and started treating me good. She would feed me and take care of me, but the standard of taking care in your world is different in our world. Taking care of someone in our world is setting them free. That is why animals, as you call us, are always trying to get away. That is also why we came back to our world. Some animals take human form, but that only lasts a while, so they must hurry back to this world before they change back to their authentic form. I don't know why this works like that. That little girl whom they sold me to was her." He pointed to Aly.

Mom and Dad remembered right away that they had bought Aly a hedgehog when she was a little girl.

Mom asked, "That hedgehog we bought her was you?"

"Yes, that was me," answered the hedgehog.

Dad was still curious about something the hedgehog said and asked him, "So you say animals that have taken a human form have to hurry back before they change back?"

"Yes," answered the hedgehog.

Dad knew that this explained the owl that had a human face. Aly looked at Dad and thought the same thing about the walking stick. Mom and Zeke remembered the javelinas, and EJ and Manny remembered the dog.

Then the hedgehog broke the silence, "I have a bitter rival that can explain everything to you and maybe how to get back, but he took off and won't be back for a while. He knows all these things. If you ask him nicely and do all that he asks, he might even guide you back."

"When will he be back?" asked Dad.

"Well, there is no telling. He went to your world and hopefully he will return. Until then just be happy that the vicious antibodies (VABs) have not come back," said the hedgehog.

"What are vicious antibodies?" Dad asked.

"You don't want to know, but I will take you to my rival when he returns and he will explain it. Goodbye." And he disappeared under the log.

CHAPTER 7

ZEKE'S DISCOVERY

After the family's conversation with the hedgehog, the family headed back inside before it got dark. Dad went back to trying to find their way back. Mom and Aly sat in the living room and discussed how weird all this was. Manny and EJ were fighting over a bag of chips. Zeke went to his room and played with his iPad, also trying to make sense of what he had just heard. Soon, he fell asleep, and he had a dream. In his dream, the family was back home; and everyone was doing their usual ritual of watching TV or, in Manny and EJ's case, fighting for either food or toys. In his dream, there was a gentle tap on his window. Zeke got up to see what it was, and it was Thor gently tapping the window with his tail. Zeke thought he was just wagging his tail, as most dogs do. But then Thor signaled with his head for Zeke to come outside. Zeke thought it was coincidence until Thor did it again. *Whoa!* thought Zeke. *How cool!* So he went outside with Thor.

When he was standing next to Thor, he signaled again for Zeke to follow him. Zeke followed, and Thor wanted to show him a dead squirrel which was lying on the lawn.

"Did you kill that squirrel, Thor?" asked Zeke. Thor just wagged his tail. "Man, you really let him have it, boy," said Zeke. "Why did you kill him?" asked Zeke.

Finally, Thor spoke to him and said, "It wasn't me. Since he was being a nuisance, the vicious antibodies got him." Zeke got scared and ran inside to tell Mom. When Mom saw him, she asked if he was okay. Zeke told her that he wasn't.

Mom asked him, "Why? What happened?"

Zeke was so scared that he couldn't talk. Mom told him to calm down and gave him a Coke.

Finally, when he calmed down, he said, "Mom, you will not believe me; but Thor just spoke to me, and his voice sounds like Dad's."

Mom told him it was not good to have such an imagination.

"But, Mom, he really spoke to me about the dead squirrel," said Zeke.

"Zeke! Zeke! Zeke!" he heard. It was Mom trying to wake him up. He finally woke up and forgot where he was and told Mom that in his dream, Thor had spoken to him.

Mom just nodded and said, "Seems to be the thing nowadays, baby, but it's okay. You are awake now in the land where animals speak. Geez! This is crazy."

Mom had dinner ready and everyone sat down to eat.

Then Zeke asked, "If we are still here by Thanksgiving, are we going to eat a bird that talks?"

"No!" the entire clan said at the same time.

So Zeke went outside to practice on the tennis courts. As he was approaching the courts, there was a big elk lying close to the courts.

Zeke had not seen him until the elk said, "So this is what a virus looks like!"

Zeke looked up and just took off back home, but the elk caught up to him.

"Please don't hurt me. I didn't mean to wake you up!" screamed Zeke.

"Calm down, Svirus. I will not hurt you. All I want is to look at you and figure out what all the fuss is about you viruses being here," said the elk.

Dad heard Zeke screaming and headed to the rescue. "Zeke, are you okay?"

"I think so," said Zeke.

"Oh, you must be the Uvirus of the bunch," said the elk.

"What do you mean?" said Dad.

"Well, the leader, the boss, the head honcho," said the elk with sarcasm. About then, the elk went "Ouch!" as a rock bounced off his head. "What the!" he said.

Just as everyone turned around, EJ and Manny were standing there with more rocks in their hands.

"You don't mess with our daddy and brother, mister," said EJ.

Manny agreed, "Yeah, what he said."

Dad went over to them and told them it was okay so they didn't need the rocks.

"Are you sure?" asked EJ.

"Yes, son, I'm sure me and Zeke can handle this," said Dad.

"Okay, call us if you need us," said EJ, and off they went back toward the house.

"Let me apologize for that. Are you okay?" asked Dad.

"Yes, I am, but everyone is not scared of you; but they should be not scared of those two," said the elk.

"Not scared?" asked Dad.

Then he remembered how backward this world was, and he apologized one more time.

"Can I answer a question?" said the elk.

"Sure," said Dad.

"Why do you have several Sviruses at one time?" asked the elk.

"What do you mean?" asked Dad.

"Well, you being one of the Uviruses means you must be like me. I am a UAB, but we only have one SAB at a time, so all our attention is focused on it. How do you focus your attention on four?"

Zeke jumped in and said, "Our Dad and Mom give us a lot of love, to each one of us."

"That's a rather common concept," said the elk. "Now, why did you think I would hurt you? I am not one of the VABs," said the elk.

Zeke asked back, "What is a VAB?"

"*Oooh*! Let me tell you about those guys. Mr. Host loves them because they end viruses," claimed the elk.

"Does that mean they will eliminate us?" asked Zeke.

"Yes, if you are their target. There are distinct types of viruses, and you are only one of them. As for the other viruses, some are good, and Mr. Host likes to keep those. I know little about how it goes, but I had a friend who was a different virus from you. He never got eliminated until he went back to wherever viruses come from. His color was a little different from yours. He was my bitter rival, but then he went back to where he came from, and I never saw him again," said the elk.

"So, by bitter rival, you mean your friend?" asked Zeke.

"No, he was not my friend. I disliked him very much! We were always together as two," said the elk.

"You know, in our world, everything you just said would be backward; but I am understanding some of your world," said Zeke.

Now, what intrigued elk was how much this Svirus knew about the world he came from.

"So tell me more about your world," said the elk.

"Well, let's start with the viruses. In my world, they know us as people. There are all kinds of people, short, tall, skinny, fat, white, brown, yellow, red, and black. There are friendly people and mean people, people who care about others, and there are some who don't care about others. We have leaders that we call politicians, and the people elect them to be leaders, but some are the biggest liars and they don't care about the people. We have four seasons—spring, summer, fall, and winter. Spring is warm, summer is ridiculously hot, fall is cool, and winter is cold. Me and my family were going for a trip when we saw this blinding flash of light and we ended on the side of the road. We don't know what happened. We had never seen animals like you talk, and we don't know why you call yourselves antibodies. In my world, 'antibodies' is a medical word used to describe cells that fight infection. Viruses in my world are the dangerous guys who infect people, but some viruses are good for people. I don't like your world because everything is backward to us. We have seen no other people except for Ramon, Ramona, Leilani, and Isabela. They live in the next house from us, but they don't come out because they are afraid of you," said Zeke.

"Why are they afraid of us? The ones they should be afraid of, and you too, are the VABs. They will get you, if you let them," said the elk. "I wish I could explain to you about our world, but I may have a hard time explaining in reverse so you can understand me. To us these ways are normal. If I say something you understand, stop me and I will explain. Okay, I just caught myself. If you don't understand, stop me. I think I might dislike, I mean like, this translation. It sounds like, like, like fun, there. So let me try. I don't know what that flash is, but it happens I think when Mr. Host runs out of VABs. Then he must replenish them, and it takes a while, but they will come back; and you and your family need to know this. Some antibodies have left this world or are trapped in your world, the same way you got trapped here. I have never been to your world but have heard from some of those that have. I wish my friend were here to explain to you how this works. He belongs in your world but lives as if he was in this world. He told me once that his kind were always taking care of their world, until another virus, or people came and started destroying it. He said that those people were vicious and wanted to take everything from Earth and took without asking. One day he will return, and he may explain it better. Well, I must stay now, but I will not come back because I do not enjoy talking to you. *Oops*, please let me translate that. I must leave now, but I will come back, because I enjoy talking to you and you do not seem menacing at all, *like those other two*! What are they called?" asked the elk.

"They are my brothers," said Zeke. "They do not leave their young ones to be eaten by other animals. They will fight. What do you deer do when a lion attacks? You haul ass and leave your young to be eaten. Well, as you can see, we don't."

"Are they from the same brood?" asked the elk.

"What is a brood?" asked Zeke.

"Never mind. I'll explain it when we talk again," said the elk.

Zeke started walking back home with Dad, and they were discussing what had just taken place. They wondered who the person was who could cross this line at will and if they would ever find their way back to where they belonged. They also talked about how Zeke had described their world, and Dad told Zeke how proud he was of him. Then they talked about EJ and Manny, two kids who would not take crap from anybody. They started laughing while they had their arms around each other's shoulder. It had been a while since they had a good laugh. Zeke also talked about how he was starting not to worry too much because the family was together and how he thought this family could get through anything, no matter how hard it would be, because of the love that they had for each other. Dad again told Zeke how proud he was of him and that he was right about this family's tenacity to overcome.

When they got home, Zeke told everybody what had just happened. Everyone was listening without blinking an eye. He also told them about EJ and Manny, how they smacked that elk with a rock. Everyone broke out in laughter and then talked about how long it had been since they had talked and laughed together.

CHAPTER 8

THE GREAT RUMBLE

After being in this world for what seemed like years, the family was growing accustomed to the ways here, which were all new to them. Aly wished she could be back home with friends, clubs, and parties. She could sometimes visit friends in Austin. All that was gone from her. Mom missed going shopping at big stores and cooking in her kitchen. Dad missed taking Zeke to tennis practice and school—even all that had been gone for a while since the world got stricken with disease. Zeke missed going to school and talking with friends and the teachers. He missed his iPad, playing video games, and playing with his Beyblades. EJ missed his bed and watching TV. He enjoyed cartoons and kids' movies. The only one that seemed happy was Manny, because he was with Mom, Dad, Aly, Zeke, and EJ. He mentioned nothing he missed. Dad would look at Manny and think, *About the joys of being a kid, no worries, as long as the family is together.* One day EJ was bored, and the shows on TV were boring to him. They were all a unique kind, all different, but he missed the ones he used to watch back home. So EJ and Manny went outside, and Dad went with them. Once outside, they ran around and played, while Dad kept a watchful eye. Dad was sitting on the big rock outside while he kept watch. Before he realized it, he had fallen asleep, and EJ and Manny wondered off further and further. When he woke up, they were nowhere to be seen. Dad jumped up; and when he couldn't find them, he went into panic mode and called

Mom, Zeke, and Aly to come help. They all started looking and could not find them. Finally, Aly saw their small footprints on some soft dirt; and everyone spread out and started heading in that direction, calling their names.

Meanwhile, the boys walked and walked, and soon they got lost.

Manny cried, and EJ tried to comfort him, "Don't worry, little brother. Your big brother will get us out of this."

"What will we eat now?" asked Manny.

"We'll find something, Manny," said EJ.

They could not find the direction they came from and EJ worried too.

"You are going the wrong way," they heard a voice say.

They both turned and could see no one.

"Who said that?" asked EJ. "We can't see you."

EJ blinked his eyes to see better, but no luck.

"He's over there," said Manny. "Under the grass."

EJ walked toward the sound, and it kept saying, "Come closer. I will take you back."

EJ and Manny didn't like the sound of the voice, so EJ got a big rock and told Manny to get one too. As they got closer, they saw the biggest rattlesnake ever, hiding in the grass. They didn't know what it was, but instinct told them to get away. The snake had just eaten a rabbit and was now after the boys.

EJ said, "Why are you trying to harm us, Mr. Antibody?"

The snake poked his head above the grass and said, "Have you ever heard of a vicious antibody?"

EJ said, "No."

"Well, I am more than an antibody. Mr. Host sent me here to eradicate you viruses," said the snake.

"What is eradicate?" asked Manny.

"It means to take all of you out," answered the snake.

"Is that why you killed Mr. Rabbit?" asked EJ.

"Yes, because they infect Mr. Host too," said the snake.

As the snake came closer, EJ got ready with the rock, and so did Manny.

EJ looked at Manny and said, "Okay, Manny, let's pull a closer on this guy. You ready?"

Manny said, "Yes, I am ready."

So they separated, and they approached the snake from both sides.

This made the snake nervous.

He said, "What are you doing?"

"We will teach you not to mess with the power of ME, dingbat," said Manny.

"Who is the power of ME?" asked the snake.

"Manny and EJ," said EJ.

The snake backed off in a hurry, with EJ and Manny in hot pursuit. He noticed that their eyes were getting bigger as they approached him, and he was trying to turn and run; but EJ and Manny had him surrounded, and he knew that if he turned, he was toast. He tried to talk them into stopping, but they were having none of it.

Finally, the snake said, "Okay, okay, can we talk this over?"

"Not anymore. We tried to talk to you, and you were being a bully. Now you pissed us off," said Manny.

They continued to close in on the snake until he ran. This was when EJ took aim, and that rock struck the snake on the back of the head. When the snake turned his head because of the pain, *Pow!* Another rock from Manny got him on the side of the head. EJ got reloaded and in came another rock, right in the mouth. The snake hid under the grass and slithered away as fast as it could.

EJ and Manny high-fived. "Don't mess with the power of ME," said EJ. "Okay, now let's find our way home," said EJ.

Only now they were unsure of what direction they had come from.

"I think we came from over here," said Manny, pointing.

EJ agreed, and they started walking. They walked for a long time and recognized none of their surroundings.

After a while, Manny said, "I'm hungry."

EJ told him, "There is nothing to eat over here."

"I hear somebody eating something," said Manny.

As they walked, they found a squirrel that had a bunch of carrots. Manny asked if he could have one, and the squirrel said no.

"I am saving them for when I hibernate." The squirrel asked, "Are you two of the viruses which came from another world?"

"We are not viruses," said EJ.

"Sure, you are," said the squirrel. "I am one too."

"How do we know if you are?" asked Manny.

"Well, if they talk as they do in your world and not backward, like in this world, then you know. Viruses talk like you do, although you must beware vicious antibodies can also change their way of talking to confuse you," said the squirrel.

EJ started thinking about the snake. He had called himself a vicious antibody, but was talking like they did.

"So, if they talk straight, they are a VAB or a virus?" asked EJ.

"Correct," said the squirrel.

"What about the carrots?" asked Manny.

"Oh no, I can't because then I won't have enough to store," said the squirrel.

"*What is that?*" EJ pointed to the sky behind the squirrel. When the squirrel turned, Manny grabbed two carrots and hid them behind his back.

"Okay, Mr. Squirrel, we won't bother you anymore. We'll be on our way," said EJ.

So off they went, and when they were clear of the squirrel, they sat down and each ate their carrots.

Suddenly, the squirrel appeared and said, "*Aha*! I knew I was missing two carrots. Why did you steal them from me?"

EJ said, "Look. We were hungry, and you didn't want to share."

"That doesn't mean you can take my carrots. Now you owe me two carrots," said the squirrel.

No sooner than he had said that, a large coyote was behind the squirrel. EJ and Manny stood up and were ignoring the squirrel.

"When are you going to give me my two carrots?" said the squirrel.

He noticed that EJ and Manny were ignoring him, so he turned and saw the coyote drooling. He took off and hid behind EJ and Manny.

"I'll eat the squirrel first, and you too viruses I will save for later," said the coyote.

"Please help me," said the squirrel.

"Let's see now. Manny, you still hungry?" asked EJ.

"*Yup*," answered Manny.

"Okay, Mr. Squirrel, we will help you; but it will cost you six carrots—the two we owe you and four more," said EJ.

"What?! That's insane!" yelled the squirrel.

"Okay, Mr. Coyote, we don't want to hurt you, so we will be on our way. Have fun with Mr. Squirrel," said EJ and Manny.

"You can't do that," said the squirrel.

"Six carrots," said EJ.

"Okay, it's a deal. Just please help me," said the squirrel, shaking.

"Deal," said EJ.

The coyote jumped in the conversation, "I don't know why you are making plans and deals. Your fate will be the same. Nobody gets away from this VAB."

EJ looked at Manny and said, "Let's do the swing?"

Manny nodded and said, "Swing it is."

EJ grabbed a stick that was lying on the ground and said, "Mr. Coyote, it's not nice to mess with the power of ME."

"Who is the power of ME?" asked the coyote.

"Manny and EJ," said EJ.

Now, after all this time, the coyote was so confident that it distracted him and he never saw Manny creep up behind him.

"*Now!*" yelled EJ.

Manny grabbed the coyote's tail and ran in circles, forcing the coyote to spin. Now what the coyote didn't know was that they had perfected this technique while playing with their dog, Thor, back home. EJ started running in front of the coyote, and every time the coyote tried to turn to bite Manny, EJ would whack him with the stick on the side of the head and the coyote would let out a yelp.

EJ would yell to Manny, "Don't let go!"

Manny would answer, "Don't miss!"

The coyote got so dizzy after a while now he was easy prey for them.

He finally said, "Okay, okay, I've had enough. I promise to run away, as soon as you let me go."

"We tried to be nice to you, but *no*! The big VAB was set on being a bully and trying to eat us," said Manny.

Finally, the coyote bit the stick EJ had and started pulling; but Manny pulled on his tail, and EJ pulled on the stick. The coyote's canines got stuck on the stick, so he got stretched out and fell. With the boys pulling, Manny pulled the coyote's tail *off*! With one big yelp, the coyote took off into the tall grass.

The squirrel looked amazed at what he had just seen.

"I'll give you eight carrots, and you don't have to pay me for the other two," he said.

So they went to the squirrel's den and sat and ate the carrots.

The squirrel said, "I overheard that your names are EJ and Manny?"

"Yeff, Mr. Fquirrel," said Manny with a mouthful.

"You don't have to call me Mr. Squirrel. My name is Harry," said the squirrel.

"Nice to meet you," said EJ.

"It's getting late, and it will be dark soon. Why don't you guys stay here tonight and tomorrow we will find your way back home?" said the squirrel.

So being that Manny was already sleeping, EJ said, "Okay, but we want to start early."

"We will," said Harry.

And everyone fell asleep.

The next morning, Manny was up early and woke EJ and Harry up.

"We need to get going, because I miss our family and I want to eat breakfast too," said Manny.

So they all walked, and Harry picked up their scent, and they followed it. Along the way, suddenly the grass wiggled, and something was crawling away from them at superspeed. They looked and couldn't see what it was. Then suddenly, the grass got shorter in one spot, and all they could see were bumps on the head of a snake as it was hauling butt away from them. They all started laughing. They walked some more, and far on the horizon they saw a coyote walking, hanging his head down. He had no tail. They laughed again and continued.

Finally, they came over a small hill.

Manny smelled bacon cooking. "It's this way!" he yelled.

EJ told Harry, "For food, Manny is never wrong."

So they followed Manny, and when they got closer, Dad was sitting outside getting ready to go look for the boys when Manny yelled "Dada!" and started running toward Dad. Dad saw them; and with tears in his eyes, he yelled from the front door, "They're back!"

Everyone ran to meet them. Mom and Aly and Zeke were all running after Dad.

Dad picked both up and said, "I thought we'd never see you again."

Mom got there, and everybody hugged them.

Mom, Aly, and Zeke said, "We love both of you so much."

EJ said, "We love you too."

Manny asked, "Is breakfast ready?"

Everyone just looked at him and started laughing.

EJ said, "This is Harry. He is a squirrel and a virus."

Mom said to Harry, "Did you bring them back home?"

"Well, we kind of helped each other out," said Harry. "They saved my life, so I paid them with carrots and promised to find their tracks back home."

"Thank you so much," said Mom. "How can we ever repay you?"

Harry thought for a while and said, "Maybe I could visit and play with them every other day?"

"You are welcome anytime," said Aly.

Now a calmer Mom asked Harry, "How did they save your life?"

"Well, I was gathering my carrots for storage when they approached me and asked if they could have two carrots. I told them no, and then they acted like they saw something up in the sky. When I turned to look, Manny took two of my carrots. Then they walked away, and I followed them, because I was missing two carrots. I surprised them when they were eating them. While I was telling them they had to pay my carrots back, this VAB, coyote, got behind me without me knowing. He said Mr. Host's caregiver sent him to get rid of viruses. He said he would eat me first and then Manny and EJ later. That's when I asked them to please help me. EJ said it would cost me six carrots. Finally, I agreed, and EJ looked at Manny and told him they would do the swing on the VAB. EJ got a stick and approached the coyote like he was stalking him from the front. The VAB dropped his guard and never saw Manny approaching from behind him. Then Manny grabbed his tail and ran around in circles, and when the coyote would try to bite Manny, EJ would whack him with the stick and kept telling Manny not to let go. Manny would say, 'Don't miss.' Finally the coyote bit EJ's stick, and his canines got stuck on the stick; and EJ started pulling one way and Manny was pulling the other way. They stretched the coyote, and then Manny ripped his tail off. That's when the coyote got loose and ran away as fast as he could. On our way here, we saw him walking on the horizon, and he had no tail. So I paid them eight carrots. They ate, and we went to sleep, and this morning I followed their scent over here. We also saw a snake with a bunch of bumps on his head. He is also a VAB. EJ and Manny did that to him."

Dad and Mom thanked Harry and told him he was welcome to come by anytime, and he could explain some more about this world. Harry agreed and went on his way.

CHAPTER 9

THINGS COME TOGETHER

The next day came, and everybody was happy that they were all together again.

Dad got together with the boys and started having a wrestling match in the living room, while Mom was watching TV, and Aly was sewing something.

Dad wondered if everybody had given up about going back home and was getting used to being here in this world. Surely, they couldn't get used to this place. So Dad went to Mom and sat next to her.

Mom, who always had great intuition, asked him, "What's wrong?"

"Oh, nothing," answered Dad.

"Who are you trying to kid? I know when there is something wrong with you," she said.

"Well, your birthday is coming up, and I don't know if I can get you anything here," said Dad.

"I'll tell you what. Take the kids and pick some wildflowers and then make that my present. We'll all sing happy birthday to me. What I want is to ask Harry a lot of questions when he comes by, and I want everybody to listen and ask questions."

"Yes, I want to do that too," said Dad, "but first I want you to know that I love you, and I feel bad for bringing everybody here, but I will make it up to you and get us out of here. That I promise you."

"You had no way of knowing this would happen, so stop feeling that way, okay?" asked Mom.

"Deal," said Dad.

About then, EJ and Manny headed for the door.

"Harry's here!" they yelled.

So everybody met Harry at the door and let him in.

"Hello, Harry!" everybody said.

"Hello, everyone," said Harry. "I came to visit, but I noticed there is a big log, lying by your house. Do you think I could move in there?"

"Nonsense," said Dad. "I'll build you a house in the spare room, and you can stay there and help us out, and we can help you."

"I would love it!" said Harry.

Mom was eager to find out what Harry knew about this world, so she asked, "Harry, can we ask you questions about this world, since they consider you a virus like us?"

"Yes," said Harry. "I can start with what I know, and then you can ask, and it might refresh my memory."

"Okay," said Mom.

"Okay, this is what I know since I have been alive. Not a lot of things get explained to us since we are viruses. They consider us to be from your world. There is some boundary between these two worlds. Some say it is the same world, only viruses act different and their way of thinking about the world is completely backward. In this world, and I told this to EJ and Manny, you can tell who a virus is and who an antibody is as they talk. Viruses must talk like you, what your version of things is. Antibodies say everything backward, from what you are used to. Vicious antibodies have the capacity of talking either way, because they claim that Mr. Host's caregiver wants them to explain why you are being disposed of and by whom," said Harry.

"So are there others like you that are considered viruses even though they are not human?" asked Mom.

"Yes, there are. I don't know how many, but I know of some. Rats, ferrets, and wild hogs. For starters, the claim is that they destroy the body of Mr. Host. I don't know of any others," Harry answered.

"So, if they destroy things, we consider them a virus?" asked Mom.

"Yes, like locust, they produce nothing but destroy crops and other plants. They only become food for other species. Have you ever met the elk out here? He has a friend that came from your side of the world, but they were a different virus. They praised Mr. Host and tried to keep his world clean and taken care of. They would only eliminate viruses and antibodies when they needed to eat or to make something that they would use. Somehow, they got outnumbered by the other viruses and were taken prisoners, and their part of Mr. Host got taken away and confiscated. I used to listen from a tree, when the elk and him were having conversations, and this is how I know this," said Harry.

Dad jumped in and said, "Me and Zeke met this elk. We could tell he was an antibody as he talked."

"You know his friend's color is almost exactly like yours," said Harry. "Maybe you know of him."

"I would have to hear his name," said Dad, "and you don't know it, so it would be hard to tell."

Mom still very curious asked Harry, "So these vicious antibodies, or VABs as you call them, do they have names, like you and I?"

"Some of them pick a name to confuse us, but all their actual names are numbers and sometimes letters. I heard that Mr. Host's caregivers give them these names. Why don't we look for the elk and ask him more questions?" said Harry.

"Okay," said Dad, "but only I will go with you."

"I want to go too, Dad. After all it was because of me that we met him," said Zeke.

"I think that would be a splendid idea if Zeke went with us," said Harry.

"Okay, but you will stay close to me all the time," said Dad.

So the next morning, they went off to find the elk, with Harry leading the way. Mom, Aly, EJ, and Manny stood outside and wished them luck and told them to be careful and then watched them disappear into the horizon.

"When will they be back?" asked EJ and Manny simultaneously.

"They will be back soon," said Aly.

"Can we wait for them outside?" they asked.

Mom said, "Me and Aly will stay out here with you guys for a while, but when I say it's time to go in, we go inside, okay?"

Again, they answered, "Okay."

So they all stayed outside for a while, until out from behind the rock jumped a big cougar. He stood there and watched as Mom, Aly, and the boys just stared back. Mom and Aly froze with fear, and the boys continued playing.

"EJ, Manny, start walking toward us," said Mom.

The boys were so involved in their game with the water hose that they ignored her. As Manny was running because EJ was chasing him with the water hose, they ran closer to the cougar.

"EJ, Manny!" yelled Mom again. "Get over here!"

So, when EJ turned toward Mom, he accidently sprayed the cat's face with a big flow of water. The water went into the cat's mouth, nose, and eyes. The cat took a giant leap backward and then started pawing his face and tumbling on the ground.

When he got up, he said, "This is my lucky day, two viruses for the price of one."

EJ looked at Manny and said, "The big kitty doesn't like water, like Thor."

Manny ran and got the other water hose; and they started walking, stalking, toward the cat. The cat stood its ground thinking they would back off, but when they didn't, he got nervous and took small steps backward. When he saw that they were not backing down, he got ready to lunge at them.

EJ said, "Okay, Manny, he will jump, just like Thor."

Manny said, "Yeah, just like Thor."

As the cat lunged toward Manny, he turned his hose right on the cat's nose. EJ ran around behind the cat and hit the other end, and we all know where the water went! The cat put his tail between his legs from the chilly water hitting his rear canal, and that screwed up his lunge. He started sneezing and blowing water out the other end. The cat lost all body control, and the boys took advantage of that! Sometimes the cat would sit and get hit by water in the nose. When he would bend down, he would get a stream up the rear canal.

EJ told Manny, "Look, Manny. He is doing the seesaw."

"Yeah," said Manny, "let's do it faster so he can seesaw faster."

Finally, the cat just lay down and covered his face with his paws and his butt with his tail.

EJ said, "The kitty doesn't want to play anymore, and it is getting boring."

While Manny kept the water stream straight at the cat's face, suddenly, this big rock bounced off his head. "Ouch!" growled the cat. The cat moved his paws to cover his head, and a big stream of water went up his nose. When he covered his nose, another rock would bounce off his head. This went on for a few minutes, until the cat made a run for it.

EJ looked at Manny and said, "He did the same thing the skunk did, back home."

They both laughed and walked back to Mom and Aly, who still stood frozen.

Finally, Mom's fear left, and she told them, "Do you guys know that he could have killed you?"

EJ said, "Naw, he didn't know he was messing with the power of ME."

"Who is the power of ME?" Aly asked.

"Manny and EJ," said Manny.

Meanwhile, while all this was happening, Dad, Zeke, and Harry had found the Elk and had a conversation with him. The elk told them he would look for his friend and bring him to their house so maybe they could figure out how to get home. Dad, Zeke, and Harry were excited on their walk home. On their way home, they saw a wet cat walking with water coming out both ends. They said to each other, "That guy looks like he is sick, like he has diarrhea or something, and he has some whelps on his head too!"

"That is one of the VABs, from around here. They come often, but they never look sick like that," said Harry.

"Well, this one does," said Dad.

They all laughed and continued home.

When they got home, EJ and Manny were asleep. Mom and Aly were in the living room. Dad, Zeke, and Harry walked in; and you could hear a pin drop.

"What happened?" asked Dad.

"You will not believe this, so sit down while we tell you," said Mom.

"That bad?" asked Dad.

"Worse," said Aly.

"Those two scared the hell out of us. After you all left, they wanted to stay outside and play. So me and Aly stayed outside with them. Then this big cougar came out of nowhere and said, 'I get two for the price of one.' He was looking at the boys. The boys were playing with the water hoses wetting each other, and they never saw the cat. Me and Aly were yelling at them to come with us, and they were ignoring us. They kept playing, and EJ accidently got water in the cat's face. The cat jumped up and started wiping its face with its paws, and that's when the boys saw it. Instead of being afraid, they called it a big kitty. They each got a hose, and Manny was aiming for the cat's nose, while EJ went behind it and started aiming at the cat's butt. Finally, the cat lay down and covered its face with its paws and its butt with its tail. Manny kept the water going at its face. Then suddenly, we heard this cracking noise, and this rock bounced off the cat's head. The cat let out a growling scream and covered its head with its paws. Then Manny would shoot water up its nose. Ehen it covered its nose with its paws, another rock would bounce off its head. It looked like the cat was playing peek-a-boo. The boys call it seesaw, and then they were laughing and saying, 'Lets' make him seesaw faster.' That's when the cat took off. They were laughing at it, and EJ said, 'You don't mess with the power of ME!' When Aly asked them who was the power of ME, they said Manny and EJ. That's when we came inside, and me and Aly have been trying to recuperate since; and they just fell asleep, as if nothing happened," said Mom.

Harry jumped in and said, "That cat is lucky they didn't take its tail off, as they did to the coyote."

Zeke asked Dad, "Hey, Dad, you don't suppose that..."

"Yes, it was son," said Dad.

"What?" asked Mom.

"On the way back, we saw this big cougar walking by. There was water coming out of every body orifice he had, and then we saw these big whelps on its head, and we all thought he was sick, with diarrhea and vomiting," said Dad.

"He looked real sick and disoriented," said Zeke.

"He looked like a sprinkler," said Dad. They all couldn't help but laugh.

CHAPTER 10

PUT TWO AND TWO TOGETHER

After all the action and disbelief that Mom and Aly had seen with the cat, Mom and Aly started thinking things weren't as tough as they seemed around here. Everybody talked about an enormous game, but if EJ and Manny could whip some butt like that, imagine what two adults could do. Mom was feeling more and more comfortable. She weighed all that had been happening: They get paid to live in this house; they get paid when they would buy anything; their car never seemed to run out of gasoline. Everyone was obviously afraid of them. Everyone talked backward from what they knew. They might be okay until they would find their way back. So, after a few hours of pondering all this, the only thing Mom disliked was the fact that nobody really knew anything and they could not get straight answers. So Mom and Aly followed the power of ME method. They became aggressive so maybe somebody would open up. Their first target was Harry, but being aggressive with him was not nice, because he tried to help. So on to the next target.

They kept talking about where to help Dad. Mom decided that she and Aly had stood by long enough and now it was time to join in the fight to find the way back home. But who would be such a target? They thought about it long and hard, and *bingo!* There it was.

They would go after that poodle, but they had to think of a way to bring her here. They slept on it and produced a plan in the morning.

The next morning, as they were eating breakfast, they discussed their plan with everyone; and Dad and Zeke said that they hadn't thought of it that way, but they thought it was an excellent plan. Aly was to go outside by herself several times a day, and the poodle would come along. Aly would invite her inside the house, and then Mom would take care of the rest.

Every day for the next few days, Aly would sit on the log and act depressed. The hedgehog would complain about it, and Aly would say, "Go away. You're next." This made the hedgehog nervous, and he apologized, but Aly would act like she didn't want to hear it. This went on for about four days. On the fifth day, Aly went through the same routine, and suddenly she heard that squeaky voice again.

"Why do you look so happy?" asked AB5, the poodle.

"I am just depressed because I don't have any friends...no rivals," said Aly, hoping that the poodle would fall for it.

"I can be your rival," said the poodle. "I asked my carrier, and she said as long as you keep your distance from them, it's okay."

Aly answered, "Too bad. I mean too good."

The poodle came closer and asked, "Why is that a splendid thing?"

Aly said, "Because back where I came from, I had this antibody rival, and I had bought a lot of food that he hated and forgot and brought it with us. That is so good! I should be ashamed of myself, but I want to do something bad now and give to another rival to enjoy, or hate it. It is a food made especially not for antibodies like you."

The poodle came closer and said, "Well, I guess it would not be all right if I had some."

"It's in the house. Let me get it."

"You mean it's outside the house and you're going to take it in, right?" asked the poodle.

"Yes," said Aly, "I won't be right back."

"Okay," said the poodle, AB5.

Aly brought some smashed crackers with canned sardine juice that Mom had mixed, knowing that dogs couldn't resist it. The poodle gulped it down in a second and wanted seconds, so Aly invited her inside the house. The poodle agreed blindly and followed Aly in. Aly introduced Mom as her carrier, and the poodle said goodbye instead of hello. They fed her a little more, and the poodle was still trying to get more. Mom told her they had run out, but if they asked questions and antibodies answered them truthfully, then more food would appear magically. The poodle agreed and was ready to answer anything. So Mom took off with the questions.

"I am used to asking questions backwards, so can answer the questions backward?" Mom asked.

"Will food disappear if I do?" asked the poodle.

"Absolutely!" answered Mom.

"Okay, then don't. I mean ask. Is that how I need to answer so food will appear?" asked the poodle.

"Yes, exactly like that," said Mom.

"How old are you?" asked Aly.

The poodle concentrated on her answers and asked, "Do you want to know how long it has been since I left my carrier?"

"Yes, that is exactly what we mean," said Mom.

"I am twenty-one years away from my carrier," said the poodle.

"What?!" exclaimed Aly. "If you lie, the food will not appear."

"Okay, for every year in time away from my carrier, it counts as seven years," said the poodle. "So my age as you call it is twenty-one. Can you excuse me for a minute? I need to go outside," said the poodle.

"Do you need to relieve yourself?" asked Mom.

"Yes," answered the poodle.

Mom took advantage of this time to explain to Aly that dogs would age seven to one in their world, and so it was the same in this world. She also noticed that the numbers increased in this world, as they had back home. Mom also found that all the names were numbers and they sounded like some medical terms. There were antibodies and viruses, and she wondered if there were any named bacteria.

Aly agreed to everything Mom was finding out. Suddenly the door opened and in came the poodle again.

"Did any food appear while I was away?" she asked.

"No, not yet. We have more questions before that happens," said Aly.

"What else do you want to know?" asked the poodle.

"Does your carrier talk to viruses?" asked Mom.

"Yes, she does, but only viruses that live nearby," said the poodle.

Mom and Aly decided that the poodle did not know much about what they were asking. The answers they were getting were coming from the equivalent of a seven-year-old child. Aly fed the poodle. The dog was as happy as she could be and said goodbye to Mom and Aly and started on her way. Now Mom and Aly had to concentrate on their next victim. After a few moments, they thought of the hedgehog. He was an adult. Aly went back to the old log and stomped on it again, and out raced the aggravated hedgehog.

"You again!" he complained.

"Yes, it's me again, and I am gonna keep doing this until you give us some explanations," said Aly.

"I don't have time for this," said the hedgehog. "I need to get my rest! Don't you understand that?" He crawled under the log again. Again, Aly kicked the log, and again the hedgehog came out; and this time he was even angrier. "I am warning you. If you don't stop this, it will force me to use my quills on you," he said.

"Ooooh, I am so scared," said Aly.

"Okay, what do you want from me, so you will leave me alone?" asked the hedgehog.

"Me and my mom need some questions answered, and you are the one we want to ask; and if you don't agree, we will force you out and let the squirrel move into this log," said Aly.

"Okay, if I answer all your questions, you will leave me alone?" he asked.

"Yes," said Aly.

The hedgehog agreed, and Aly called Mom and told her he had agreed to help them. So they both started their interrogation.

"Are you a virus or an antibody?" they asked him.

"You can't tell when I talk? I am a virus," he said.

"You have lived in our world and this world. What is the difference? And we want a straight answer, not about you knowing someone that knows someone that knows someone. We want straight answers about what *you* know," said Aly.

"Okay, you may not like what I have to say, but here goes. Both worlds are almost identical. Same viruses and antibodies in both worlds. In your world, your kind of viruses dominates and destroys as they live. In this world, you are a second-rate virus, because there are viruses that make you look harmless. That is where most of the VABs spend most of their time, destroying these viruses. I am considered a virus too because I lived in your world for a time. I have heard that there are three other viruses that are here, and they are familiar with you," he said.

Right about this time, Ramon, Ramona, Leilani, and Isabela showed up during the conversation. They had finally ventured out of the house, though they were still nervous about this unknown world. They asked if they could sit and listen in and lose their fear of this land. Mom and Aly told them they were more than welcome to listen.

"Okay, keep going," Mom told the hedgehog.

"As I was saying, there are at least three other viruses close by familiar with you. They were in your house, in your world. I will tell you how to find them later. If we have lived in your world, they consider us viruses no matter whether we destroy Mr. Host or not. You want to know who Mr. Host is? I assure you that very few antibodies or viruses in this world know specifics on him. We know he has a caregiver that oversees sending VABs wherever they need them. Antibodies get named according to their strength rating, starting from 1 to 10, with 10 being the strongest. They rate the VABs on a unique system. We rate them different because their major purpose is to disguise themselves, and that makes it easier to approach and destroy viruses they look for. That is all I know, and I am being perfectly honest with you," said the hedgehog.

Mom looked at Aly and said, "Okay, we'll leave you alone, but if you remember anything else, we need you to tell us, or Aly will come and visit you again."

"I'm kind of liking you guys now," said the hedgehog. "Maybe we can keep on sharing information."

"We like you too," said Aly, "and we can visit whenever I come out here."

"I would like that," said the hedgehog.

Mom and Aly went back inside and talked about the information they had gotten from the poodle and the hedgehog. They figured they needed to get somebody from this world or, as they referred to themselves, antibodies. The talk about Mr. Host was really frustrating for Mom because she was tying the names, numbers, and other things she was hearing to the medical field. Mom and Aly were not the type that would give up that easily, and they would keep searching for the truth. When they walked inside the house, they sat down, and the entire family came to join them. Ramon, Ramona, and their kids had a very confused look on their faces. They talked about what they had just heard from the hedgehog and wanted to know how Mom and everyone in her family found out that these animals could talk. They asked if they knew yet why they referred to themselves as antibodies. Mom and Dad shared all the information they had, but it made the other family nervous. They decided they would go back to their house and continue staying inside until it was safer. Mom and Dad discussed this after they left, and their nerves were frustrating. Sometimes it felt like they were not willing to help.

Dad told Mom that there was no need in forcing them to help unless they wanted to. Otherwise, if they did not commit fully, they might commit errors and compromise the goal. Mom agreed, and then she asked about who else they could talk to that would answer some of their questions. Dad suggested they make a list of all encounters and see which one would have the more beneficial answers, since they should not raise suspicion on what they were doing. The complete family got together and started their list and discussed why they thought their choices' answers would be useful.

"We have already asked both of my candidates, and they were not much help. They just added more questions," said Aly.

"You never know all that information the hedgehog gave us may help link other information together," said Dad.

Everyone worked on the list. When they finished, Mom and Dad went through it and started noticing a trend. Each name had a number at the end. They decided this was a suitable place to start—find out what this number meant. Now in the medical field, antibodies had a number and some letters for identification. They applied the backward theory, and they found that the antibodies were numbered according to strength. Once finished with the list, Mom and Dad looked at it and asked questions about everybody's choices. First, they asked Aly.

"Do you think we should ask more questions to those two or maybe ask differently? Or what do you suggest?" asked Mom.

"I think for the poodle, I should convince her to bring her mother one day, and maybe we can get more answers," answered Aly.

"Okay, how can we do this?" asked Dad.

"Well, we bribed the daughter, so maybe we can do the same with the mother," said Aly.

"We have plenty of time on our hands, so see if you can think of something we can do to make that happen," said Mom.

"Okay," said Aly.

Next up was Zeke.

"I think we should go to the elk and invite him here, where we can all ask him questions," said Zeke.

"Do you think he would answer or be reluctant since he is, or it seems, a devout antibody?" asked Mom.

"I think he will answer. It just depends on how we ask," said Zeke.

"Okay, your task is to figure out how to get him here and how to ask the questions," said Dad.

"I can do that," said Zeke.

Mom decided that would be enough for now. Dad agreed.

"How about us?" asked EJ.

"The way you guys beat up those guys, I don't think they would answer anything for us," said Mom. "You guys need to stop doing that to these critters, even though you may not like them."

"But we only got rough with them because they were trying to harm us. If they were friendly, then we would be friendly too, like Thor. We play with him, but don't hurt him," said EJ.

"Yeah," said Manny.

"Okay, who do you think will answer our questions and help us out?" asked Dad.

"How about Harry?" said EJ and Manny simultaneously.

"Harry has already been helping us," said Mom. "Pick somebody else."

"Okay, how about that bear at the store?" said EJ.

"Okay, we will try him too," said Dad. "But I need both of you to promise that you will stop being that aggressive."

"Deal," again, EJ and Manny said simultaneously.

"So everybody has something to plan on. Take as much time as you need. We should be in no hurry on this one," said Mom.

Everyone agreed about what their tasks were, and they knew that there was no hurry. The only hurry was to make it back home safely and together, not necessarily in that order.

CHAPTER 11

THE CLAN ON OFFENSE
(ON THE ATTACK FOR NON-SPORTS FANS)

The morning started slowly, with everybody waking at different times. Mom just waited to cook breakfast until everybody was up. Dad walked groggily into the kitchen and headed straight for the coffeepot. He filled up his cup and, looking perfectly happy, sat in the living room to enjoy it. Mom got her coffee and went to the living room with Dad. They started wondering if anybody were missing them back home and if anybody would look after they saw nobody home for a lengthy period. Surely Mrs. Lerma would notice they were not there and report it to the police. Mrs. Lerma was kind of the local FBI informant and neighborhood watch expert. She was a pleasant lady, but watchful. So, surely, she would notify somebody when she saw them gone for a long time.

One by one, the clan came to life. Manny was the first one, and he demanded to know if breakfast was ready. Aly followed, and she too went straight for the coffeepot. Now the only late sleepers, and hard to get going in the morning, were Zeke and EJ. So Mom sent Manny to wake them up. Soon all the complaints against Manny could be heard all the way to the kitchen. EJ and Zeke finally made it to the living room couch and took a quick nap. As soon as the smell of bacon hit their nostrils, they came to life. Manny was already at the table with a fork in his hand, desperately waiting for breakfast.

Mom always cooked a damned excellent breakfast, so everyone was eager. Little by little Zeke and EJ started inching toward the table. Once everyone was at the table, Mom broke the ice by asking if anybody had their plan ready.

EJ started the conversation, "I think I should get a haircut."

"How does that fit into your plan?" asked Dad.

"My hair is too long and curly, and I think it is blocking my thinking," said EJ. "If I had short hair, I bet I could think better."

"EJ," said Dad, "we don't know if anybody around here gets a haircut or if there are any places that cut hair here."

"I can cut it with Mom's scissors," said Aly. "I know I can do it."

"Can you cut it right?" asked Manny. "Because I want it cut too, but after you cut EJ's."

"Why do you want EJ to go first?" asked Zeke. "Why don't you go first?"

"Because EJ and you are my older brothers and I am supposed to follow your example," answered Manny.

"I think you just don't trust Aly and you want to see how it works on EJ before you let her cut yours," said Zeke.

"I'll even cut your ears off!" joked Aly.

Manny made a series of strange faces, and everybody started laughing at him.

"Okay," said Dad. "Did everybody think about their plan? We want to hear from everybody whether or not you did. Okay, Aly, you go first."

"I have been thinking about it. I am stuck because the one I wanted to interrogate produced nothing worth using. That hedgehog confused me more than anything. I think I will ask him to bring the two he mentioned. You know, the ones he said that knew us. Hopefully, they are smarter than him and can relate more helpful information to us. I haven't figured out how I will do this, but it'll come eventually," said Aly.

"How about you, Zeke?" asked Mom.

"Oh! Hi, Mom!" said Zeke. "I am still thinking of the elk and how I can get him to explain things or commit to bringing that friend of his to talk to us. He thinks we are interesting viruses, so I

73

am gonna try to get him to think this is a game. First, I'll dare him to talk backward, which will be our way, and we can understand him better. He wanted to talk to me and Dad, but he thought we were backward. I'll tell him that in our world, talking backward is a sign of high intelligence. I am sure he will fall for it. The problem will be to find him because I haven't seen him out by the tennis courts. He mentioned that he was only there because he wanted to see what all the fuss was about us viruses. After we eat, I will go out there and see if he is around. I know he wants to be around us out of curiosity, and that is what I will use to my advantage," explained Zeke.

"That sounds like an outstanding plan!" said Mom and Dad. "Hopefully, you can find him out there. He seems like he will be easy to convince if he thinks he is being viewed as intelligent."

"EJ, how about you?" asked Mom. "Are you and Manny gonna do this together?"

"Yes, we are, but we need our haircut first so we can think better, because all that hair won't be in the way," said EJ. "Aly says she can cut it, and we will let her do it."

"Who are you going to go ask, after your haircut?" asked Dad. "Maybe Harry can help ya'll."

"We will ask Harry when he comes back if he knows anybody that wants to play with us. While we play, we will ask them questions," said EJ.

"Yeah, and if they don't answer, they will have to deal with the power of MEZ!" said Manny.

"Wait a minute, young man!" said Mom in an angry tone. "What do you mean by that?"

"Well, they are all afraid of us, and we can scare them into telling us," said Manny.

"You will do no such thing, the both of you. You will be friendly to all animals. If you don't like them, then stay away from them, but I don't want to see you two start any more aggression. You will be friendly and respectful to everyone. Do I make *myself clear*?!" said Mom.

"Yes, ma'am," said all three boys at the same time.

"By the way, what is the power of MEZ?" asked Mom.

All three boys just looked at each other. Finally EJ answered, "Manny, EJ, Zeke."

"That will come to end as of today, okay?" said Mom with a lot of authority.

"Yes, ma'am," again all three said at the same time.

"Can I say something?" asked EJ.

"Go ahead," said Dad.

"I wanna say that me and Manny are not mean to animals when they are nice to us; but when they get mean, then we get mean, because we don't want them to know that we fear them. With Thor it is different because we know he won't hurt us and he loves us and he knows we won't hurt him," said EJ.

"Yeah, I wouldn't pull Thor's tail off," said Manny, "or put water up his nose. We only put water on him because he is hot sometimes and it feels good for him."

"I don't throw rocks at him either," said EJ.

"Goats are a different story. They smell bad. I won't hurt them, but I won't go near them," said EJ.

"Yeah," said Manny.

"Okay, if you promise then, I will make a big cake for all three of you," said Mom.

"Yay!" all three yelled.

"Now, it's time to hear Dad's plan," said Aly. "What is your plan, Dad?"

"My plan includes that bear at the store and Ramon," said Dad.

"Where does Ramon come in?" asked Mom.

"My plan is brilliant if I may say so myself. I will convince Ramon that me and him have a bet on the bear. The bet will go like this: I bet that the bear cannot speak backward because he is not that intelligent. Also, he does not know a lot about his surroundings; therefore, he is ignorant. That is why he wears a hat so nobody can see that he can't think. From my experience with people who act like that, as soon as you challenge their intelligence, they spill their entire world to you, trying to convince you they are not dumb. Before he even realizes what he has done, we will have a lot more info from him. The major problem will be to convince Ramon to play his part, but I think I can do that. Well, there it is. What do you all think?" asked Dad.

"It sounds difficult, but I know *you* can do it," said Mom.

"*Go for it, Dad!*" all the kids joined in.

"Now, let's hear Mom's plan," said Dad.

"I was afraid of that," said Mom. "Since I have had no encounters, I wouldn't know where to start."

Everyone was quiet and looking at each other for a while.

"I know what Mom can do!" said Zeke out of nowhere.

"What?! What?!" yelled everyone.

"Mom is so good at keeping records. She pays the bills, saves money, has everything in order, and keeps our home rolling. In all actuality, she saves our lives every day. Especially when EJ and Manny lose my stuff, Mom finds it for me. She is a supermom. She can keep records of what we find out, and then we will have all the information together, and she will figure what to do," said Zeke.

"*Wow!* That is outstanding!" said Dad and Aly at the same time.

"Go, Mom!" said Manny and EJ.

Everybody's function was ready. The plan was in place. Now it was time to put it in motion. Mom was happy that she didn't have to go out and deal with these critters, and that was exactly why she understood what EJ said about goats. After breakfast, everyone went to the living room and discussed their plans. Zeke felt like he was going on an outstanding adventure like the ones he had seen on one of his video games. He was thinking to himself that he could do this, and he had not felt like this for the longest time. He could visualize himself talking to the elk and accomplishing his goal. He was feeling unstoppable. He realized what this meant for his family, and he hoped that his plan would be the one that would take his family back home. Aly was thinking about how to get the hedgehog to feel like he had to get to his friends and bring them here to talk, but make it sound like he wanted to do it. She thought everyone had talked about challenging someone. Then that approach would surely work on the hedgehog. Dad sat there staring into space, also wondering how his biggest problem was convincing Ramon to help and sound serious about their bet. He knew that the proud bear would fall for their plan, because he could not stand a challenge to his intelligence. Now if only Ramon would help, Dad knew this would work. Mom was just thinking how happy and proud of Zeke she was for him producing that idea. She never wanted to meet these things, much less on their grounds. EJ and Manny were happy to be going outside.

CHAPTER 12

SURPRISE, SURPRISE!

Everyone was busy getting ready to put their plans into action. Mom enjoyed a quiet cup of coffee and relaxed on the couch. She was thinking of cleaning the kitchen after everybody left. Her plan was to clear the sink counter first and then move on to the rest. As she got to the counter, she saw it was dark in that small area, so she spread out the curtains. To her surprise, there was a big beautiful butterfly flying around and sucking out the juice from the flowers on a bush right under the kitchen window.

Now Mom had always liked all these colors and shapes on butterflies. She opened the window, completely forgetting that she was in an unfamiliar world. Through the open window, she started admiring the colors and shape of the wings of the beautiful butterfly. She was in a trance as the butterfly went from flower to flower; it was like the butterfly was performing a beautiful dance. As the butterfly got closer to the window, Mom said to herself aloud, "What a beautiful dance you are performing." The butterfly came closer and changed flowers at a faster pace. "You seem so free and happy," said Mom.

"Why are you saying I am beautiful? What did I ever do to you?" asked the butterfly.

Mom heard this, and it paralyzed her for a moment. Then she thought, *Wait. I know this is happening. It happened to everyone, so I am not crazy.*

"Why are you saying I am beautiful? Did I do something right to you?" asked the butterfly again.

Mom then snapped and remembered where she was. *I must use backward meaning*, she thought. "Yes, you did something very wrong," Mom said.

"Whew! I was not worrying already," said the butterfly.

Mom thought to herself, *Wow, this is what all the kids and Dad have been talking about, backwards stuff.* "You are the most horrible thing I have ever not seen," said Mom.

"No, thanks," said the butterfly, as she landed on another flower.

"Can you not stop flying so I cannot see your colors?" asked Mom.

"As soon as you stop being impolite and not face me when you talk to me," said the butterfly.

Mom remembered everyone talking about this, and she turned her back when she talked to the butterfly. "Do you know how to talk backward, like a virus?" asked Mom.

"I cannot try. I have always done this," said the butterfly.

"Is it hard for you? I guess it would be for anyone," said Mom.

Mom could not stop looking at the beautiful colors on its wings; she became mesmerized. She would remember times in the past when she would look at butterflies when she was a little girl and just admire the wing colors and how fragile they seemed to be. She also remembered how they became a beautiful butterfly, from a not so beautiful caterpillar.

"Let's try talking backward," said the butterfly.

"Okay," said Mom, "let's see what I can ask. How long were you a caterpillar?"

"I was a caterpillar for not very long. I cannot remember those days," said the butterfly. "My carrier discussed none of that with me, so I never knew."

"Do you remember spinning a cocoon?" asked Mom.

"No, I only remember coming out of one," answered the butterfly.

"Wow, you spoke backward perfectly!" said Mom.

"Sometimes things come easy to me, but I had never tried this," said the butterfly.

"Okay, in our world it is impolite to talk to somebody when your back is to them. You want to try facing each other before we talk?" asked Mom.

"Yes, we can try that too," said the butterfly.

Mom was thinking about asking a lot of questions, but something told her she might want to start a little slower and kind of make the butterfly relax and divulge more information. Then she thought about how a beautiful insignificant insect like that could hurt anything. So she figured she would start off asking trivial questions at first and then move on to more detailed questions about what everybody had set out to do.

Now, Mom being as trusting and polite as she had always been with everyone, said, "My name is Yolanda. What is yours?"

"I am FAB10," said the butterfly.

"Why does everybody have a number and letters for a name?" asked Mom.

The butterfly hesitated to answer and then reacted, "I don't know. It is just our names are given by our carrier."

Mom noticed the hesitation and thought to herself, *Why did she hesitate at that moment? She was just trying to talk backward, or was the butterfly trying to hide something?* Then she thought there could be no way that this beautiful insect could have any malicious intent. Surely she was just confused at talking backward, which would cause any human, even the most intelligent ones, to think about what they would say.

"Where do you live?" asked Mom.

"Among the flowers," answered the butterfly. "I spend my life just flying and gathering food from flowers."

"So you never sleep?" asked Mom.

"I sleep among the flowers too. We can't see at night. So we have to stop and sleep among all the flowers for protection," said the butterfly.

Mom had not noticed that the hours had passed and everyone was returning home. She cooked dinner for them. Dad, Zeke, EJ,

Manny, and Aly walked in; and everybody collapsed somewhere, on the couch, in chairs, on the floor, and everywhere else they could. When dinner was ready, Mom called everyone to the table, and she noticed Harry was with the guys and he too collapsed on the floor. So she got a small bowl of peeled pecans and told Harry that she welcomed him back. When they all sat on the table, Mom mentioned that it had been a long time since she saw everyone sitting at the table and that she liked that. Everyone looked indifferent since they were all starving.

"I wonder if we will ever get to eat at McDonald's again?" said Zeke.

"Whenever we get back home," answered Dad.

"Yeah, whenever that is!" said Aly.

"Soon," said Mom, knowing that nobody even had the slightest clue when that would be.

Everyone talked about their day and wondered if they got anything accomplished. Dad and Zeke could never find the elk, even with Harry's help. Aly said the hedgehog never came out, even though she jumped on the log and rolled it. EJ and Manny had been with Dad and Zeke, so they were not even worried about what was going on. Finally, after seeing everyone depressed, Mom told everyone about her day.

"Well, as I was looking out the window, I saw the most beautiful butterfly I have ever seen. It had the most beautiful colors, and it went from flower to flower, so I had a conversation with it. She told me her name was FAB10. I introduced myself, and we talked about where she came from, and she had no trouble talking to me straight instead of backward. She said she didn't remember when she was a caterpillar, only when she emerged from the cocoon. It was a friendly conversation overall," said Mom.

"What did you say the name was??" asked Harry.

"FAB10," said Mom.

"No!" said Harry. "Did you give her any information about your family?"

"Like what?" asked Mom.

"Well, how many in your family, male or female, and adults or children?" said Harry.

"No, the conversation didn't go that far. That was when everyone started walking in and I cooked dinner, and I don't know if she is still out there. Why are you asking me this, Harry?" asked Mom.

"Well, if I am right and remember right, that is one of Mr. Host's caretakers, detecting vicious antibodies. They fly around and pretend to be friendly, while they are getting all your information, so that more VABs can come looking for you," said Harry. "These antibodies report back to the caregiver, so he can send the VABs after you. They are deceiving, but there are two ways to tell right away."

"How?" asked Mom.

"One way is that they have no problem talking like viruses. They can talk either straight or backward with no difficulty. Another way is whenever you ask a personal question about them, they cannot help but hesitate," said Harry.

"She hesitated. When I asked how come all their names are letters and numbers, she said that their carriers are responsible for their names," Mom said.

"See, I bet her actual name is FVAB10, which means flying vicious antibody. She hesitated because they are so programmed that they have to think every time they are about to lie," said Harry. "Good thing we came in when we did; otherwise, she would have tried to get a lot more information from you."

"But how can something so beautiful be so dangerous?" asked Mom.

"To draw you out and then report back to Mr. Host's caregiver, so he can send more after you," said Harry.

Everyone was quiet at the table now. Finally, EJ and Manny broke the silence. "We won't let them hurt anyone, Mom. We can handle this."

Mom said, "I know you guys can. I am not afraid. I am just mad now that it would take advantage of me. But one thing the butterfly doesn't know is that you don't want to piss me off. I am going after it and won't stop until we catch it and get a lot of information from it. You want to play rough? Bring it."

Zeke looked at Dad and asked, "Tennis racket time?"

This was the method used at home to kill hornets and any other flying insects that flew in and bothered them back home.

"Exactly," said Dad. "Here's the plan. Boys will go outside, and we'll hide behind the flower bushes. Aly and Mom will pretend they got hypnotized by the butterfly. Zeke will have the racket. When we surprise him, we need to make him fly toward Zeke, guys. Then Zeke can bring him down with the racket. EJ will have the jar, and that's where she is going. Zeke, how's your forehand these days?"

"Never been better, especially when you mess with my mom!" said Zeke.

"Can we step on it after we catch it?" asked Manny and EJ.

"No," said Mom, "we need it alive so we can get some answers. That thing doesn't realize that she messed with the power of ZAMMED."

"What is *that*?!" the clan asked.

"Mom, Manny, Aly, Dad, EJ, and Zeke," said Mom.

There was a resounding "*Yeah*!" from everyone.

CHAPTER 13

THE RETALIATION BEGINS

They executed the plan. Mom and Aly went to the window. Dad and the boys hid behind the bushes. When everyone was in place, Mom pretended to tell Aly about the butterfly, while Harry was under the sink waiting to hear every word. Harry was advising them what to ask.

"When she shows up, ask her how long she has been an antibody," said Harry.

"Okay," said Mom.

"Aly, I wish you had seen this butterfly. It was beautiful. It had huge wings with dazzling and beautiful colors. It had me hypnotized for a while with its grace and beauty," said Mom aloud.

"I wish it would come back, so I can see it. I want to get hypnotized too," said Aly.

Before they knew it, they could see the butterfly flying toward the flower bushes again. It started away from the window and then gradually came closer. All this time Mom and Aly were commenting on how beautiful it was.

Dad whispered to the boys, "Get ready. When I give the word, let's get it."

Finally, the butterfly was right outside the window and said, "Hello, Yolanda, who is with you?"

"You have to confuse her," whispered Harry. "Tell her Aly is your son."

"This is my son," said Yolanda.

"Don't you mean your daughter?" asked the butterfly.

"No, my son," said Mom.

"Ask her what her carrier's name is?" whispered Harry.

"What is your carrier's name?" asked Aly

"Keep asking more personal questions," whispered Harry.

"Why is your name in numbers and letters?" asked Mom.

There was a big moment of hesitation from the butterfly.

"Now!" yelled Dad.

The surprise stunned the butterfly, and it froze. Zeke executed a forehand that even the greatest tennis players would envy. *Zap!* Down came the butterfly, and EJ pounced on it with the glass jar. Dad put the lid on, and they had her in the jar.

"You can't do this!" yelled the butterfly.

"You have been ZAMMED!" yelled Manny.

"*Yes*! You just got ZAMMED!" yelled Mom.

"What is that?" asked the butterfly

"Zeke, Aly, Mom, Manny, EJ, and Dad," said EJ.

They took the butterfly inside, and Dad asked Mom to do the honors. The butterfly looked really surprised when Mom and Aly approached the jar.

"Why are you doing this, Yolanda?" asked the butterfly.

"You tried to make a fool out of me, and that is not nice. I will show you what fairness is. We don't want to hurt you, but we want a lot of information from you. You say you want to be free. I will give you the chance to free yourself. The lid on this jar comes off after ten turns. For every twenty questions you answer correctly, I will turn the lid once. When you answer all the questions we have, the lid may be off, and you can go," said Mom. "And don't trick us, because we are well aware of your defects."

"What if I refuse?" said the butterfly.

"There is a big spider web outside, and I am sure a big spider lives there," said Harry.

"You wouldn't do that," said the butterfly.

"Yes, I would, because you are the one that reported my family and the big antibodies caught them," said Harry.

The butterfly just stared at Harry and asked, "Why are you helping them when you know that Mr. Host's caregiver will find out?"

"Because Mr. Host's caregiver classified us as viruses because we came from their world, as an accident, like they did," answered Harry. "And we all want to go back to that world."

"Okay, first question," said Mom. "Why do you have letters and numbers for a name?"

The butterfly hesitated and said, "Because our carrier—"

"You are lying," said Mom. "For every lie I will tighten the lid more."

"Okay, okay," said the butterfly. "We don't come from a carrier, or cocoon, like you were asking. They create us from chemicals, and those chemicals used give us our names."

"They make you from chemicals?" asked Aly

"Yes, they make us from chemicals. In your world, you call us pills, tablets, shots, medicines, and/or treatments."

Everyone got confused, and this brought out more questions.

"Why are you after us?" asked Dad.

"Because you make Mr. Host ill, and his caregiver must eliminate you. You refer to his caregiver as a doctor. He sends us to come and eliminate you."

Mom was now putting everything together, being she was deeply knowledgeable in medicine. All along she had felt that the names they had heard from these things were medical terms.

"So do you consider yourself an excellent thing or bad?" asked Dad.

"I don't consider either. I am programmed to take care of all viruses. That is why there is a 10 in my name. It is the symbol of a scavenger antibody that will search everywhere for you," answered the butterfly, "and then report back to the caregiver, who will decide on how to eliminate you from Mr. Host's system."

"Who is Mr. Host?" asked Mom.

"I am not sure, but from what I know, he is the being where we all live in," answered the butterfly.

"Then you say that we live inside someone's body, and that is this entire world?" asked Mom.

"That is any world, whether far or near. I know there are many worlds where there are other antibodies traveling too. If you really want to know more, contact the elk. He has a friend that travels often between what you call your world and this world. Our VABs have been trying to capture him for a while, but he has evaded us for a long time. I am telling you this, because we are not to be captured like this. We should be way smarter than you viruses, and you should not outsmart us like you did me," said the butterfly.

"If I let you go, will you tell the caregiver where we are?" asked Dad.

"Yes, I have to. It is my function here," answered the butterfly.

"Well, then we have to keep you here. We will feed you and try to keep you comfortable. I hope you understand why we can't let you go, until we figure out a way out of here," said Dad.

"I wish I could say I would not let them know, but I have to," said the butterfly.

"We can't take a chance," said Dad.

Mom and the entire family agreed that they could not let the butterfly go. She also told them that her strength as an antibody would diminish by half every day, so she might not last long. Mom and Dad talked about it and decided that they would release her and take a chance, especially if she got weaker by the hour. Night came along and everybody went to bed; but before falling asleep, the butterfly was on their minds. The thought of living inside someone's body just sent chills through their bodies. When morning came and everyone was getting ready for breakfast, they heard someone knocking on their door. Dad went to answer, and when he opened the door, the elk was standing there with Harry.

"I finally found him," claimed Harry.

"I think I found you," said the elk.

Mom and Dad asked them to come inside. The elk seemed scared at first, but Harry convinced him that all was okay. He came in and looked nervous. When Dad asked him why he was nervous, he told Dad that they never should have captured that FVAB10. Dad asked why.

The elk explained, "These high-level antibodies they send to find you viruses. If they find you, they will report back and disclose your location. But if you confuse them, they cannot pinpoint it. But if they get captured or die, then the caregiver can pinpoint exactly where they went missing. So we must confuse him and then release him, so he can't pinpoint exactly where you are."

"Why do you refer to her as him?" asked Mom.

"There is no such thing as a female antibody," said the elk.

"But she talked like a girl!" exclaimed Mom. "And what about the poodle that came to Aly? She sounded like a girl."

"They do this to disguise themselves. When they are hunting viruses, they are neither male nor female. They activate by several ways. The caregiver is responsible for their activation," said the elk.

"Why are you trying to help us?" asked Dad.

"Well, because Harry is my friend. He has taught me how to speak the way you viruses do. I am considered a safe antibody, like some bacteria that grow along the bank of the red river," said the elk.

"What is a safe antibody?" asked Mom.

"One that does no harm, or help. Basically all we are is food for the antibodies," answered the elk. "I am waiting on my friend to come, and he will explain it all. He is very good at this," said the elk. "It is hard for me to talk backward, but I have been practicing; and no, I am not a VAB that can talk both ways. I have been learning from Harry and I like it."

The elk asked everyone to excuse him for a few hours, so he could go find his friend and bring him to the family, so he could try to explain by telling them all he knew. For the first time in a while, the family felt like they were getting somewhere. Dad and Mom told the elk to do that. They realized, for the first time, that a lot of the inhabitants here were looking at them like leaders into something. Dad asked everyone if anybody had seen Ramon's family outside their house or anything. Dad had not spoken to them since they planned to go see the bear. Everyone knew that they would stay in the confines of their house, where they felt safe. Dad invited them over so they could hear what was going on and they could offer their ideas too, since they were in this together. When he got to their house, they opened the door and seemed nervous. Dad explained to Ramon and his family what had been going on, and they were all happy about what they heard. They explained how fearful they were about all this, but now they were little by little getting over it, and it was about time to help. Dad explained that even though it was dangerous, together they could overcome anything. So Ramon's family was now excited to come over and join the fight. Ramon and his family told Dad that they would come over in two hours. So Dad headed back home and waited for the elk and his friend.

CHAPTER 14

THE REVELATION

D ad got home and asked everyone if the elk was back. Everyone answered with a depressed "no."

"That's odd," said Dad. "I wonder if the elk is okay."

About then, there was a knock on the door. Everyone got quiet as Dad answered the door. It was Ramon and his family. They had a bunch of groceries with them.

"Can we cook here?" asked Ramona.

"Yes," said Mom. "Help yourself."

Ramona headed for the kitchen to put away the goods, and Mom followed.

She explained to Mom what they had been doing and how they were coping with all this. She said they were afraid of all their surroundings and that they had been at home all this time, except for a few times they would all walk outside together. Mom told her they too were afraid, except for the boys and Aly helping with trying to figure how to get out of here. Ramona was all ears, as she listened to Mom explain what had gone on. Finally, there was another knock on the door. Again you could hear a pin drop. Dad went to answer the door, and everyone could see he had his fingers crossed. When he opened the door, there stood the elk and his friend. His friend was a Native American, and he had a friendly-looking face. Everyone was excited now that they would find out about everything that was going on.

"Hello," said Dad.

"Hello," said the man.

"I am Juan," said Dad.

"I am Fidelio," answered the man.

"Welcome," said Dad.

"Sorry I could not get here sooner, but I had some stuff I had to take care of," said Fidelio.

"You can get us out of here?" asked Ramon.

"Well, it may not be that easy; but yes, I think we can. It will be a process," answered Fidelio.

"Can we offer you something to eat?" asked Dad. "We eat great around here."

"Yes, I would like that very much," answered Fidelio.

The elk said he had a few things to do and he would return tomorrow. Everyone said goodbye and thank you for everything, and he went on his way. Mom and Ramona had already been cooking, so the food was ready. All the adults sat on the table, while the kids found distinct places around the living room to sit.

"I guess I can start while we eat," said Fidelio. Everyone agreed, and the kids moved in closer so they could hear. "Did everything start with a giant flash?"

"Yes!" was the answer from everyone.

"I too came here by accident, such as you did. I went through the same dazzling flash and the buzzing sound. I could never find my way back. I have traveled throughout this crazy world for many days. The animals here think I can go from this world to our world at will, but that is not the case. I have prayed to my ancestors a lot during this time of trial. They have tried to show me the way, but a lot of what they show me I cannot understand. It seems to be from another time and it confuses me. I will tell you what they have shown me, and maybe together we can return safely to our world. Let's start from the beginning. Have you ever wondered where in the sky we really are? That has always been a question that everyone has always ignored. Even the greatest minds in the world, in my time, ignored this. Is it another dimension between what you know as our world and this world? Is it another plane that this exists on? Or is there a distinct reality where we are? All the people in the world will accept other explanations, except the one I am about to tell you. Since the dawn of time, our ancestors have been looking to the skies for answers. Seldom did they find any. But they assumed that this was going on, never really sorting this out. The solution has been staring us in the face, but all through time we could never see it. Can you believe that there is no other world, as you thought before? Can you believe if I tell you it is the same world? That the only difference is that now you are more aware of your surroundings, that now you hear what animals say, and that they do the same? You are in the same world, which can never change. My ancestors showed me that the brightest minds talk about time travel and alien visitors, and everyone is ready to investigate whether it merits it. There are so many theories of people seeing this and people seeing that, and so many people believe in these things that nobody has even bothered to see where our reality comes from. We see storms only as a change in temperature that gathers condensation and wind and wreaks havoc on us. But is that all they really are? People are so busy making a living and worrying about the day that all the important things go unnoticed. They are so busy being managers, wondering where they will be in one year in the company they work at, and they worry the worst about politics. Lately this has gone awry, and nobody does anything to stop it. Would you believe me if I told you we are part of a larger being and that he or she may be part of an even bigger being? All things reproduce from one thing into a bigger one.

For instance, there was once a man who worked for NASA. His job was to develop pictures coming in from satellites. The older people here probably remember that back then, pictures had to get developed, unlike now where you can take a picture and it instantly appears. The man went on vacation to a beach on the eastern shore. While he was walking on the beach, he saw a bunch of little crabs running around and mostly away from him. He took a picture of one of the little crabs. When he got back home, he had forgotten to develop the film. So the man said to himself, 'When I go back to work on Monday, I'll take my film and develop it during one of my breaks.' He finished his vacation and returned to work on Monday.

When he was on one of his breaks, he remembered his film and developed it. When he hung it out to dry, he saw some negatives he had developed for NASA hanging on his line. The pictures were mostly of the eastern seaboard. He looked at his negative and wondered where on that huge shoreline he was when he took the crab picture. So he blew up his negative and lay it over the NASA negative and tried to see if he could find the spot. After he blew his negative up, he laid it on the NASA negative, and he was in for a shock! The small blown-up negative lay right over the shoreline, and it followed every indentation on the NASA negative. It was as if he had laid the same picture over it. He couldn't believe it, so he did it again. Again, it matched perfectly. He got so scared that he hid his pictures and he told nobody about it, because he knew that people would think he was crazy. Had he investigated it, he would have made the discovery of the century or of all time. He would have found that we are inside a bigger being. Now is he like us? No one knows. To better arrive at what he would have found, we must look at all the surrounding similarities. One example is ants. There are exceedingly small ants, mid-size ants, and big ants. Yet we don't even think twice when we see one. It is an ant and they all look alike. Maybe distinct colors, but they all look, well, like ants.

So what does our solar system resemble? An atom. Planets revolving around the sun, just like electrons revolving around a nucleus. The nucleus being made of protons and neutrons. Could these emit energy that we don't see or refuse to see because we think it is not important? Could they emit energy like our sun that we refer to as sunlight? These electrons each circling in their own orbit and never colliding? Sounds familiar? We hear about a black hole, and we dismiss it as odd and dangerous. Could it be a tube leading to somewhere? We live on one electron and never even looked closely at this. Earth, Venus, Pluto, Mars, Jupiter, Saturn, Uranus, Neptune, and Mercury are electrons of the sun. The average number of electrons is nine or ten. Didn't they just discover another planet on the very outskirts?

If this is the reality, then that would explain why we are considered viruses or an illness, because we invade, destroy, and then move on to greener pastures. We already have our eyes on Mars. Could this be why our universe is growing? This explains the big bang theory. This giant being is growing, and as it grows, things just get farther apart. Being that a group of atoms form a molecule and a group of molecules form a cell and a group of cells form a tissue, think about it. Several solar systems form a galaxy, and several galaxies form a universe. What do several universes form? We may never know. Could it be that a group of solar systems form a molecule or galaxy, a group of molecules form a cell or universe, and a group of cells or universes form a tissue? We may never know what a group of universes form. Could it be organs or what we know as nebulae?

So if this is the case, are we a disease that invaded this organism and, after almost ruining Earth, we are looking to Mars as our next victim? All these things, known as a disease to us, are antibodies being taken by this enormous being to rid its body of us. Every time we clear a stretch of South American Jungle, an unknown disease emerges and is fatal to us, until we develop a vaccine. Are the vaccines we develop an immunity to these antibodies? Or something that allows us to mutate and become immune to the antibodies? Immunity from these antibodies this giant being has taken? As we know, after a certain period, disease that affects us develops an immunity sometimes.

Disease is coming out of more and more strange places than ever before. Now it is even transferring from animals to humans at a rate never seen before. Are all these diseases, as we call them, some medication that this giant host is taking to eradicate us? Unique people affect Earth in unique ways. First, there are people who want the resources from Earth to get rich, so they plunder the land in search of any resource that can be sold. They sit on the land even if it doesn't belong to them. They take without asking and cannot be trusted anymore that you can pick them up and throw them. At one point, they even forced people to work for them and then made excuses why they did that. Are these people one kind of disease?

Second, there are the people who kind of follow the same rules, except they don't take without asking. These people are more hard-working but very head strong with some things. These are the people easy for medication or antibodies to work on because of their nature. They feel that they are indestructible that they would not seek help.

The third kind of people are bent on just complaining about their poor luck and how they could have done better had it not been for the first kind of people holding them back.

The last are the people who lived off the Mother Earth, only taking what they needed to survive. This kind would be the harder to eradicate because they are strong survivors. They have survived through the harshest conditions, but never thrived because of their anger at the first kind of people.

There are four distinct types of people that could be four types of disease, which are ailing this giant being, known by the animals as Mr. Host. They don't know his or her name. They just know that they are like medicine taken by this being, and the moment they hit a certain fluid or system, they come to life. They are meant only to fight what ails this being, programmed to destroy viruses and bacteria harmful to this system. We cannot say exactly what triggers this taking of medication. Is it an action taken by humans that causes pain or discomfort that the need for these antibodies is required?

Younger generations are seeing this, and they are trying to correct this, but for the wrong reasons. They are looking for fame and niches, no matter whose expense. They are more interested in who is watching them do this and not doing it for the benefit of mankind.

We see this in all aspects of everyday life, nowadays. News people who would rather report on their opinion than the actual happening. Young CEOs of enormous companies, who feel if we need a product, then that gives them the right to raise the price to an outrageous level, for example, medications, not caring if the people in need can afford it. Just the fact that they will buy it regardless, they take it as a right to raise the price, but nobody sees this because it's only old people who need it. Well, they can't face the fact that everyone will be old one day and go through the same.

To correct this behavior, everyone would have to do some dehumanizing, and that is impossible. So we must learn to live in it, and we have become immune to this behavior, because we are too busy trying to get rich or famous, with as minor work as possible.

So, after everything you now know, let's summarize: We live in a world, which is about to explode, with all that is going wrong today. Our world is within somebody's cell system. They consider us an illness, and the medication taken by this someone results in what we call a disease. A disease to us is medication to the host. Every time this being takes a certain medication, it results in a disease for us. This medication kills a lot of us, until we develop a vaccine to counter its effects; and we develop an immunity to this medicine and continue our path of destruction, until another medicine comes by and then the cycle starts all over again. We get diseases that live in a world much smaller than ours, and we take medicine to defeat these diseases. I wonder if the diseases in our body see the same thing we see in our bigger host. Remember the guy with the satellite picture? Where things are the same, but you don't know it until you get a bigger picture.

Now that you know where you are and why, we need to work on getting you back where you are more comfortable not knowing all this."

Having heard this explanation, the two families seemed dazed and mesmerized about what they had just heard. Some thought it might be true, and others were skeptical, but one thing they all agreed on was that they did not belong here and they were ready to get back to their version of reality.

CHAPTER 15

DAD'S PREPARATION

Having heard the most amazing theory of what and where they were, there was a long moment of silence from everyone. Manny broke the ice, "When do we eat?" as Manny was always hungry, "Manny! We just ate, it is not time to eat again," said Mom.

"What are we going to have for dinner?" asked Zeke. "What I wouldn't give for a nice hamburger, from you know where."

"Sorry," said Mom. "Meatloaf will have to do."

"I like meatloaf," said Manny.

"What don't you like?" asked EJ. "You eat anything."

Meanwhile, Dad was talking to Fidelio at the door and invited him to join them for dinner also, and Fidelio agreed.

Dad also invited Ramon and Ramona and their children, and they all agreed to eat together again.

Fidelio's explanation had taken a few hours, so time for dinner was close.

While having dinner, Fidelio explained how they could get out of this place safely. "The way will be a little tricky," said Fidelio.

"We must reproduce the light flash or be ready for when that light flashes again," he continued. "I will try to find out when the flash will return, and we need to be at the same spot where you were when it flashed the first time," he said. "This way, we know exactly where you are and are able to return home," said Fidelio.

"But how will we know this?" asked Dad with a puzzled look. "What if it just flashes at unfamiliar places and times?"

"This is what I must find out," said Fidelio. "What were the events that led to the flash?" asked Fidelio.

"What do you mean?" asked Mom.

"Well, I know there is always a series of strange events, which happen before the flash," said Fidelio.

Dad jumped in and asked, "Strange like what?"

"There is usually a series of strange events, which happen before the flash. Something in those events knows exactly when that flash will occur again," said Fidelio.

"A day before the flash, while driving, everyone was asleep, and I saw this big owl flying toward us. When he flew over the car, I saw his face was a human face. I freaked out and for a while I thought I was seeing things, but then when we got here, I realized it wasn't my imagination," said Dad.

Aly joined the conversation. "We were at a restaurant in the mountains, when suddenly there was a walking stick on my leg. The waiter put a napkin over it and carried it outside. Everyone thought I feared the walking stick, but I was more scared that he also had a human face."

"And what about the javelinas?" said Mom and Zeke at the same time. "We threw some food out so we could get in the car, and they took off running and I heard one of them say, '*Run*! Get away from the viruses!'"

"What about the dog at the restroom?" asked Manny and EJ.

"What dog?" asked Fidelio.

"We went to the restroom at a gas station, and there was this dog lying outside the door," said EJ. "We really had to go, so we pushed him with the door out of the way. Then we could hear him scratching at the door. So I got done first and went outside, and the dog kept making fun of me and Manny and sticking his tongue out at us. I told him to stop that, and he said 'Make me.'"

"That's when EJ got mad and kicked him in the nuts," said Manny. "Because he would not stop."

"After I kicked him, he took off and called us an awful name and would stop and lick his nuts and then take off again. He was a mean dog," said EJ.

Fidelio could not help but laugh at these two. "So you are the ones I have heard of?" he said. "Every antibody is afraid of you two, even some vicious ones." "We have to find all these animals and ask them to tell us how they know when the flash will occur," said Fidelio.

"But wouldn't that be next to impossible?" asked Mom.

"Maybe, but we have to try it, because that is my only way out of here too," said Fidelio. "I have been trapped here for a long time. I need to get back to my family too. What year did this happen to you?" asked Fidelio.

"What do you mean?" asked Dad. "It was April 2020."

"What?!" exclaimed Fidelio. "2020?"

"2020," said Mom.

"Why are you so surprised?" asked Aly.

"You will not believe this, but it was 1886 when it happened to me," said Fidelio

"That's not possible!" said Mom. "You don't look a day over fifty."

"That's how old I was when it happened, and I still thought I was fifty," said Fidelio. "Now I know I have to get back, and I wonder if my family is still around," said Fidelio, in a sad tone.

"Maybe when we go back, we go back to our own time," commented Aly.

"I sure hope so," said Fidelio. "Regardless of time, we have to find our way back. I will find those animals in that order. First, it was the owl, then the walking stick, javelinas, and then the dog, right?"

"Yes," answered Dad.

"I thought I had all this figured out, but I see there are things yet to figure out," said Fidelio. "I have been looking for a way back for a long time. I have roamed all over this world, hoping to find it, but I had no luck. As I said, all these animals thought I could cross back and forth, but I can't. It is no wonder I could not understand all the things my forefathers disclosed."

"Does the bird count?" asked Mom.

"What bird?" asked Fidelio.

"The one that told us we had to go three times the same route before we got out of there," said Mom.

"Was that after the flash?" asked Fidelio.

"Yes," said Dad.

"It would not hurt to find him too," said Fidelio. "So now I will look for this owl first and then all the other ones. Any other odd things that went on? Think and let me know when I get back. I will be back in two days."

Fidelio then left. Mom packed him a lunch, and Dad wanted to go with him, but Fidelio insisted he stay and protect the family in case the VABs were close by. Dad agreed and thanked Fidelio for helping them, and Fidelio said that this was for him too.

Fidelio went to the elk and asked if he had ever seen an owl that stayed in this area. The elk said there was one that flew by every three days, but then would disappear for a few days and then return. He was not sure if this owl would find food and then come back or what.

Suddenly, they heard this loud *Whooo!* from the trees nearby. They kept quiet, and they heard it again, but this time it was a little different. "*Whoooo* is looking for me?" said the owl.

"I am," answered Fidelio.

"Why?" asked the owl.

"I need your help to get back to my world," said Fidelio. "I need to see my family and protect them." "You have been witnessed, changing from owl to human and from human to owl on the way back," said Fidelio. "Now, you know the rules around here. If you want me to disclose who saw you, answer my questions first. Then you get to ask a question."

"I don't need a virus to explain the rules to me," said the owl.

"Well, if you don't agree, then I will bring the person who saw you, and he will have the power to make you answer any question he has, and you don't get to ask any. With me you have the option of trading questions," said Fidelio.

"I won't trade questions with a virus," said the owl.

"Okay, then I will go back and get the person who saw you changing, and he will ask, and you will have no choice."

"Then bring him, and you also know the rules. Only he can ask the questions. Once he says he is done, then his power over me is over," said the owl.

"I'm well aware of the rules, and we will return tomorrow, so I know you will be here," said Fidelio. "And, no, you are wrong. He will only lose his power if he answers one question from you."

"I will be here to free myself of that control," said the owl.

That afternoon, Fidelio traveled back to the family's house and told Dad what the owl had said and explained to him what kind of control Dad had over the owl, since he saw him change from human to owl. Dad agreed and they would head over to the owl in the morning.

The morning came quick, and Fidelio asked Dad if he was ready and said he would explain what to say on the way to the owl. All throughout the walk, Fidelio was coaching Dad what to ask the owl and to be careful what he said when he ended his questions.

Finally, after two hours, they arrived to where the owl was. Fidelio told Dad to remember everything they had talked about on the way there. Dad told Fidelio that he was ready.

"I don't hear the *Whoooo!*" said Fidelio in a loud voice.

"*Whooo* is there?" came an answer from the trees.

"I will answer him," said Fidelio. "You cannot answer any of his questions."

"Okay, got it," said Dad.

"I am back with the person who saw you change," said Fidelio. "He is right here."

"Let him speak then," said the owl.

"I need some answers," said Dad.

"How do you know it was me that was changing?" said the owl.

"I am not here to answer your questions," answered Dad. "I am here to hear answers from you."

Fidelio had told Dad that if he answered a question for the owl, he would set him free from his obligation.

"What if I don't wish to answer?" asked the owl.

"I will tell you again. I am not here to answer your questions," said Dad.

"Okay, so shall we continue?" asked the owl.

"One more time, I am not here to answer questions for you. I am here for your answers," said Dad. Surely the owl was trying to trick Dad into answering a question which would free him from his obligation, but Dad was having none of it.

"How do you know when the big flash comes?" asked Dad.

"Which flash?" asked the owl.

Dad was getting aggravated because the owl would not give up and was still trying to trick him.

"Answer the question!" said Dad.

"It comes when Mr. Host's caregiver is trying to find where viruses are attacking the most," said the owl.

"How will we know when?" asked Dad.

"When Mr. Host feels ill," answered the owl.

"And when is that?" asked Dad.

"How do you expect me to know that?" asked the owl.

"I need to remind you again. I ask the questions, not you," said Dad. "How do you know when the flash is coming?" asked Dad again.

"When the bacteria line up on the north bank of the red river," answered the owl.

"And how do we know when this happens?" asked Dad.

"When the red river turns white. You will know this because all the insects are flying toward it," said the owl.

"Where do we have to be to be reversed by the flash?" asked Dad.

"You have to be at the same place where you were when it happened to you," answered the owl.

"Why are the insects heading to the river?" asked Dad.

"They will feed on the bacteria," said the owl. "Is there anything else you want to know?" asked the owl.

"You don't give up easy, do you?" asked Dad.

"No, I wouldn't survive if I did," said the owl.

"Where is this river?" asked Dad.

"There is a hill, just past your house, with a store on it. As soon as you go down the hill, you will see the river," said the owl.

Dad remembered that was the store where the bear was at. He looked at Fidelio, and Fidelio nodded, signifying that he knew where the river was.

"Will we find a walking stick there?" asked Dad.

"If he is an insect, he will be there. I guarantee it," answered the owl.

"Will he be under the same obligation you are with me, with whoever saw him change in our world?" asked Dad.

"Yes," said the owl.

"How will we know him?" asked Dad.

"Walking sticks usually walk on the bank while all the other insects feed while flying. Very few of them have a black spot on their backs. That is a marker sign," said the owl.

"How about the javelinas? Where do they gather?" asked Dad.

"Those are easy. Just look for cactus. They love that," answered the owl.

"Do you want me to thank you for your information?" asked Dad.

"Does it matter to you?" asked the owl.

"I will still ask the questions," said Dad. "If I need anything else, I will return."

"Wait!" said the owl. "When are you going to release me?"

"I ask the questions," said Dad. "Goodbye."

Fidelio told Dad what an outstanding job he had done, but that he had never thought of holding the owl anymore, but that it was a splendid idea. Dad said that this way, if he needed the owl, he would be around hoping to be released and he could find out more information if he needed it. He would release the owl eventually. They made their way back home feeling like they had finally achieved something, and this could mean that they might be on their way home. One step closer.

CHAPTER 16

MOM AND ZEKE UP AT BAT

Dad and Fidelio walked into the house, and everyone gathered around to hear what had gone on with the owl. Dad explained to them what the owl said and they should keep an eye out for insects flying to the river. This was their first clue. Fidelio explained that they must verify what the owl said, by finding the walking stick, the javelinas, and the dog with sore nuts and asking them for more information. He explained to them they had this control over them since they saw them act differently on the other side. Dad asked Mom and Zeke that they must join Fidelio and him to find the javelinas and ask them how they crossed over with the flash and how did they know when it would be coming.

Mom and Zeke were ready to go, and after a good night's sleep, they would be even more ready. So everyone went to sleep, and for the first time in a while, Dad felt ease. Mom had a good rest, and so did Zeke.

Morning came quickly, and everyone was excited to see what they could get from the javelinas. Fidelio knew of a spot where there was a bunch of cactuses, and Dad and he were sure this was where they would find the javelinas. Off they went toward the red river, and as they were getting closer, they heard the javelinas fighting over some tender cactuses. There was a lot of racket going on, and they never heard them approaching. Next thing they knew, they were close to them.

"Hey!" yelled Zeke

The racket kept going, as they kept arguing about the cactuses.

"Hey!" yelled Zeke, louder this time.

The javelinas turned and ran, but Fidelio said, "Stop right there!" Yolanda and Zeke saw you acting like this on the other side, so now you are committed to them and need to answer all they ask."

"Okay," said the biggest javelina. "How do you know it was us?"

Fidelio looked at Mom and Zeke and said, "Don't answer. Instead ask them if it was them, and they can't lie."

"Was it you talking and running away from us on the other side?" asked Mom

"What if it was?" asked the javelina.

"Don't answer their questions," said Dad. "Just tell them you will ask the questions, and be careful because they will try to confuse you."

"Was I you on the other side?" asked Mom.

"Yes, it was," answered the javelina.

"How do you know when you will cross the line?" asked Mom.

"We count the days," said the javelina.

"How many days?" asked Zeke.

"Do you know how to count?" asked the javelina.

Zeke thought about it for a minute, and he almost answered, but he remembered. "How many days?" he asked again.

"We can only count to ten so we count to ten three times," said the javelina.

"So it's one month?" asked Mom.

"I don't know," said the javelina. "What is a month?"

"Don't answer, Mom," said Zeke.

"Hey, that is not fair!" said the javelina. "You can't do that."

Fidelio jumped in. "They can, because they both saw you. Now me and him can't," he said, pointing to Dad.

"When is your count over?" asked Mom.

"We have not finished the second one. We are on seven," answered the javelina.

"So that means it is seventeen days, so we have thirteen days to get ready," said Mom. "We are leaving now," said Mom.

"Do you have questions for us?" said Zeke.

"Yes, we do," they all said in a chorus.

"Goodbye," said Zeke, with a smirk on his face.

On their walk back, Mom asked Fidelio why these animals had to answer these questions. Fidelio said that when you witnessed these animals acting like they did on this side, then they felt surprised, and it was embarrassing to them. They didn't want their world to know that they were caught, and they thought if they didn't answer truthfully, then the entire world would find out they were caught, and that was where embarrassment came in.

Mom was thinking all along about how all these names and some actions resembled medical terms and medical procedures. She thought, *It almost sounds like Mr. Host is undergoing some treatment, which would explain the flash. The day count from the javelinas is at thirty days, which means that this flash must be some medical exam that is done every thirty days.*

As she walked with everyone, her mind was going a hundred miles an hour. She had seen so many exams being done at the hospital where she had worked that one of them had to resemble this giant flash. She figured that they must have crossed this line before the flash and they were already in it when the flash happened. She thought, *X-ray? MRI? CAT scan?* Had to be some picture to create a flash. Dad asked Mom why she was so quiet, and she told him that all this time, she thought the flash had to be some medical exam. Dad agreed and Fidelio just looked at them with a puzzled look, as he had never seen all these exams Mom was talking about.

Zeke was just enjoying himself by throwing rocks into the brush as they moved along.

When they arrived at home, it was already dusk, and they all sat around and ate a meal that Aly had cooked. EJ and Manny were happy to see Mom, Zeke, and Dad all return home.

Fidelio asked if he could sleep in the spare room, and Mom and Dad told him he was welcome to it. Before everyone went to bed, Fidelio was very curious how life was in 2020; so he started asking questions, and everyone started asking questions about his era. Some answers were fascinating to him about 2020, and his answers about 1886 were fascinating to the entire family.

CHAPTER 17

ALY ON OFFENSE

The next morning, Dad and Fidelio went outside to drink their coffee and talk. Fidelio told Dad that it was Aly's turn now, but they would have to wait until all the insects would head to the riverbanks. Dad suggested that they both go with her like they had gone with Mom and Zeke. Fidelio agreed, but worried about how they would find the walking stick, since they all looked alike. Dad reminded him about what the owl had said that there was only a few with the dark spot on their backs, so Aly would have to ask several of them until she got to the one they needed. The walking stick could not deny it if it was him, because he was under Aly's control, until she answered one of its questions.

Dad called Aly outside and told her they needed to talk to her, so that Fidelio could explain to her what to say and what not to say. Aly came outside and was all ears, because she wanted to get home badly. Fidelio started with the first part. "First, you must not show any fear of insects," he said. "No matter how scared you are of them, you must maintain your composure, for if they sense any fear, they will fly and come buzz in your ear, because they know that scares humans."

"I will try, but they just give me the creeps," said Aly. "That is the nastiest sound ever."

"You must keep your composure," said Dad. "Just remember when we lived in Laredo and all those bugs would fly around us."

"I know I can do it if I know they can't come close to me," said Aly.

"We can't promise that," said Dad, "so you are just going to block them out."

Fidelio added, "Just pretend you are somewhere else, where there are no bugs."

"There are bugs everywhere," answered Aly.

"We are just going to ignore them," said Dad.

"Okay, if it means going back home, then I will do it," said Aly.

"Can she wear bug repellant?" asked Mom.

Everyone was so focused on Aly that they didn't hear Mom coming.

"I don't see why not," said Dad. "You agree, Fidelio?" asked Dad.

"I don't see why not either," said Fidelio.

"We still have a few days before the insects fly to the river, so practice being around bugs, so you will get used to it," said Fidelio.

"That's a wonderful idea," said Aly.

The day passed by, and no insects headed to the river yet.

So the next morning after breakfast, Aly got close to the bugs so she would get used to being around them. There were big bugs and small bugs, flying bugs, and wormy insects. Aly detested them, but she wanted to go home even worse. She would push them around with a stick and make them spin, twist, turn, and roll over. Manny and EJ would come out and help her. They were not afraid of insects and would always mess with them back home. Mom went outside too and told EJ and Manny to leave them alone, since they were not doing any harm to anyone. Then she remembered the butterfly and went back inside, since she was afraid of bugs too.

This went on for three days. Aly would be around the bugs, and Manny and EJ would join her. Zeke would go out there only occasionally. Finally, on the fourth day, Aly went outside, but there were no bugs to be found. She looked up and there they were, all moving toward the river. She ran inside and told Dad and Fidelio that all the bugs were heading toward the store.

The family rushed outside and knew that it was time to head to the river.

As they walked toward the river, Dad and Fidelio coached Aly on what to say and what to look for. They told her the walking stick would ask her questions in a roundabout way, trying to trick her into answering. They told her about the control she would have over this insect, since she had witnessed it acting differently in their world, which was forbidden to do. Aly wanted to know why the insect would be committed to her.

"Well," said Fidelio, "you saw it acting as if it was in this world when it was in our world. It is embarrassing for them to be seen. They fear of you telling everybody what you saw, and they can't lie and say it wasn't them. Embarrassment to them is unbearable."

"You mean it has to answer all my questions, right?" asked Aly.

"Yes, and only you, and it can't lie. What they do is ask questions in their answers, so be very careful," said Dad. "Whenever I got confused with the owl, I would just tell it 'I ask the questions around here.'"

"Remember that," said Fidelio.

"Okay, if I am confused, just say, 'I ask the questions,'" said Aly.

"Exactly," said Dad.

As they passed the store, they could see the bear sitting outside in a rocking chair. Aly waived, but there was no response from the bear. Dad told them he was just a grumpy old bear, and they all laughed. They soon could see the banks of the river, and Fidelio mentioned that they had to get on the east side of the bank, and they were on the west side. When they got there, Dad found a low spot, and they all crossed. While they were crossing, Aly mentioned that the water was white and red underneath. Not paying much attention, Fidelio and Dad continued as they were in a hurry to get to the other side.

They finally got on the other side, and the number of insects all around them amazed them. They were flying, crawling, jumping, and who knows what else. They were all feeding on the white stuff floating in the water.

When they got closer to the area the owl had mentioned, Fidelio spotted the walking sticks farther away from the banks. They were feeding on other insects that were heading to the water. Fidelio and Dad walked to where the walking sticks were, and Aly followed close behind. She had never seen so many insects in one place. She was happy she hadn't.

They started walking over the walking sticks, and Aly spotted one with a black spot on its back. She approached it and said, "Are you the walking stick I saw on the other side?"

The walking stick just stared at her with a scared face and never answered.

Aly moved on and found another one with a black spot on its back. "Are you the one I saw on the other side?" It too just stared at her, with a piece of insect flesh hanging from its mouth. "You are nasty!" said Aly and moved on.

Aly started thinking and trying to remember any features on the walking stick in the restaurant. "Yes!" she exclaimed. "I don't think it had a spot, but I remember a crooked antenna," said Aly.

Everyone looked for the one with the bent antenna. They looked and looked until Aly saw two antennae sticking out from under a rock. She moved the rock with her foot, and out came the walking stick, trying to run away.

"*Stop right there!*" yelled Aly. Fidelio and Dad heard this and headed to where Aly was right away. "That's it," said Aly. "I remember that crooked antenna."

The walking stick stopped and looked scared, and he was trapped between some rocks and Aly. As they got closer, they noticed that he had some black spots, but they were covered with dirt.

"Did you cover those spots on purpose?" asked Aly.

"Who wants to know?" asked the walking stick.

Aly almost answered, but Dad stopped her from answering and told her to remember what they had talked about on the way. Aly snapped out of it and realized what Dad and Fidelio had been talking about.

"I ask the questions here," she said.

"Okay, what do you want to know?" asked the walking stick.

"I just told you that only I ask the questions," said Aly again.

The walking stick stood quietly and waited for the next question.

"Did you cover your spots on purpose?" asked Aly again.

"Yes," said the insect.

"Why?" asked Aly.

"I thought you would not recognize me without spots," said the insect.

"What about your bent antenna?" asked Aly.

"I forgot about my defect," answered the insect.

"I have a lot of questions for you. Are you going to answer truthfully?" asked Aly.

"Yes, I have to," said the walking stick.

"How do you know where and when to go when the big flash comes?" asked Aly.

"What big flash?" asked the walking stick.

"I ask the questions," said Aly. "How do you know where and when to go when the big flash comes?" she asked again.

"When the river turns red again, I head toward the trees and the black ribbon," said the walking stick.

"Where is the black ribbon?" asked Aly.

"It is behind the bear's cave and on top of the hill," said the insect.

"Do you mean the bear that sells merchandise?" asked Aly.

"Yes," said the insect. "How can you not know it? You came from there," said the walking stick.

"Uh-uh-uh, I ask. You answer," said Aly, waving her finger. "How will I know the black ribbon?" asked Aly.

"Because you came from there," said the walking stick.

"How do you know when to go there?" she asked again.

"I told you when the river turns red again, you wait for two days, and then the flash will appear," said the insect.

"What time do we have to be there?" asked Aly.

"There is a dog that tells us when to go. He knows time and he stands on the black ribbon, and the flash happens shortly, thereafter," said the walking stick.

"Where can I find this dog?" asked Aly.

"You have to ask the elk. He knows where the dog is all the time, because the dog always chases that elk," said the insect.

"Is it daylight or night when the dog goes to the black ribbon?" asked Aly.

"When the sun is in the middle of the sky," said the walking stick.

"Would you like me to thank you for answering all my questions?" asked Aly

"It would feel good," said the walking stick.

"Okay, I will thank you later," said Aly.

"Wait. Aren't you going to release me?" asked the walking stick.

"I ask the questions," said Aly.

Aly looked at Dad and Fidelio, and they both nodded, telling her they had excellent information and they needed to find the dog. On their way back, they had forgotten where the dog came in on all this. Then it hit them—EJ and Manny at the gas station. As they kept walking, they wondered about the dog. If they found him, was he going to fear EJ and Manny? Still, he must answer all their questions because they had that control over him. They walked back home and knew that they were one more step closer to going home.

CHAPTER 18

WE MEET AGAIN

When they arrived at home, everyone was excited to hear about how it had gone for Aly. Zeke was asking Aly a million questions, and EJ and Manny were doing the same on her other side. Dad told them to wait, and Aly would tell them all that happened over a nice warm dinner. Mom told everyone that it would be ready in about thirty minutes and that they should let Aly get some rest. They all backed off and started in on Dad and Fidelio.

Mom said, "Zeke, EJ, and Manny! Dad said wait for dinner and then they will tell us what happened."

Dinner was ready, and everyone sat on the table and was anxiously waiting for Aly to spill all the beans, as the boys called it. Dad started the conversation by telling everyone about the walk over there and the river, how it was red, and how they had to wade across to get to the side where the insects were. He mentioned about how many insects they had seen. It was enormous numbers. Fidelio added that there was a lot of white, round things floating on the river, which was what the insects were after. They had asked the walking stick what that was, but it did not know. Dad asked Aly to tell everyone about the walking stick.

"I hate bugs," said Aly, "but I had to be strong to get all these answers that make it closer for us to get out of here. He was hiding under a rock, but I saw the antennae; and one was crooked, and I remembered seeing that at the restaurant. So I kicked the rock, and he tried to run, so I yelled at him to stop and he did. He got cornered by some rocks. He had covered the dark spots on his back to keep from being found, but we found him anyway. I asked him how he knew when the flash is coming. He said they go to the black ribbon and stand there and wait for the flash. He cannot tell time, so he said the dog can, and he said the elk knows where the dog is. And that is where EJ and Manny come in."

All this time when Aly was talking, Manny had been taking food from everybody, when they were not looking.

EJ caught him and asked, "Why are you trying to take food from everybody, Manny?"

"I thought you didn't want it. I don't want Mom to get mad because you left food on the plate, so I am doing it for you, my big brother," said Manny.

Everyone gave him a dirty look because nobody believed him. Dad told Manny to stop doing that, and he and EJ had to get ready to talk with Fidelio about the questions for the dog. The boys were excited about that, and Zeke asked if he could go along too. Dad and Fidelio decided it was okay for Zeke to come along and help with the boys. Dad set up a time in the morning when they would take off and look for the elk, since he would know where they could find the dog.

The morning came quickly.

"We will start in about an hour," said Dad.

"I will pack you guys a lunch you can take with you," said Mom.

"How about something to drink too, because it gets hot and you get thirsty?" said Aly.

"We won't be away that long. Why would we need a lunch?" asked Dad. Everyone turned and looked at Manny. "I get it," said Dad.

Mom packed a lunch. Meanwhile Aly got a container where she could put something to drink, while the boys got ready to go. An hour later Dad announced that they were ready to go. So off they went, and Mom and Aly stayed outside, watching them as they disappeared into the horizon. They gave them a silent, best wish and went back inside.

As they got closer to where the elk usually was, they saw an eagle flying over them, like it was stalking somebody or something.

They then heard a familiar voice from under a large rock. "I hope it goes away," said the voice.

EJ and Manny recognized the voice instantly. "*Harry!*" they both yelled simultaneously.

"Is that who I think it is?" said the voice.

"Yes, Harry, it's us," said Dad.

"Whew, I thought I would have to teach that eagle a lesson," said Harry, as he came out from under the rock.

"Sure," said Fidelio. "We know."

"So what brings you guys out here?" asked Harry.

"We are looking for the elk," said Dad.

"You haven't heard?" asked Harry.

"Haven't heard what?" asked Dad.

"Nobody's seen the elk around here for a while," said Harry.

"Just our luck," said Dad.

"There has to be a way," said Fidelio.

"What did you need him for?" asked Harry.

"Well, the walking stick told us that the dog can tell us what time we have to be at the same spot where we were when the flash hit us, to go back home," said Dad. "He also told us that the only one that knew where to find the dog was the elk."

"You are looking for the same dog that walked around with a limp for a while?" asked Harry.

"It is," said Dad, "but now we may not find him."

"Hold your horses," said Harry. "If it's the same dog, he would always chase the elk around."

"That's the same dog," said Fidelio.

"I know where to find two critters that he always chases around," said Harry.

"You do?" asked Dad.

"Yes, they live under the biggest log. You can find if you walk that way," said Harry, pointing downhill, "but be careful, because they are good thieves. They will steal your stuff and hide it."

The boys and Dad and Fidelio walked downhill toward the huge log on the ground. Soon they could hear somebody arguing about what belonged to who.

They got a little closer, and Fidelio called out, "Hello!"

It got quiet, and nobody would answer. Harry showed up soon afterward and called out their names, "ABs, you can come out. It's okay." Again, no answer. "You can come out. Nobody will hurt you," said Harry.

Soon, a little trapdoor opened, and all anyone could see was four small eyes, looking at them.

"Hello," said Dad, "can you come out for a minute?" asked Dad. "We promise not to hurt you."

"We took nothing that belongs to you," said a little voice from inside.

"That's not why we are here," said Dad.

"Then why are you here?" asked the voice.

"We just need to find the dog that chases you all the time," said Dad.

"Okay, we are coming out, but no funny business, okay?" said the little voice.

When they came out, it was two ferrets. They looked like they were hiding something. One of them looked at Dad and could not take his eyes off him, as if he knew him. He just kept staring at him.

"I know you!" exclaimed one ferret.

"From where?" asked Dad.

"From the other side," said the ferret.

"Yes!" said the other one. "I remember him too!"

"You must not confuse me with someone else," said Dad.

"No, I remember your face. Your partner carrier took us home from this place where they used to sell us. Then after some time, this lady who was sometimes in your house took us," said the first ferret.

Then it hit Dad. "These are the two ferrets we had and gave to Mrs. Pena, who used to clean our house."

"Now I remember you," said Dad. "What a small world."

"He's harmless," one ferret said to the other.

"Why are you looking for the dog? Are you going to teach him a lesson?" they asked.

"No, we just need to get some information from him. That's all," said Dad.

"What do we get?" asked the ferrets.

"I'll give you shoestrings," said Zeke.

"Both of them?" they asked.

"Yes, both them," said Zeke.

"Give us the strings first," they said.

Zeke took the strings from his shoes and gave them to the ferrets. They sounded like they were extremely happy about that.

"Okay, the dog always comes from that direction," they said as they pointed toward the hill. "He comes from there. We heard there is an abandoned house, with a compact house next to it. That's where the dog rests," they said.

"We wanna thank you two for the help," said Dad.

Off they went toward the hill. They found the compact house next to the old abandoned house. As they approached the compact house, they heard the dog barking at them.

"Don't come any closer," the dog said.

"We are coming closer," said Dad.

"Why?" asked the dog.

"No! No! No!" said Fidelio, "We ask the questions around here."

Then the dog saw EJ and Manny.

"Keep those two away from me," said the dog.

"We will if you come out and answer all of our questions," said Dad. "Since you don't want those two close to you, I am gonna have to ask the questions for them. You agree? Okay, I'll listen to their question. Then I will ask it to you," said Dad.

"What is it you want to know?" asked the dog.

"No! No! No!" answered Dad. "We ask. You answer."

"Okay," said the dog.

"How do you know when it is time to go to the black ribbon?" asked Dad.

"That's easy," exclaimed the dog.

"Okay, so we need to know," said Dad.

"When the shadow of that branch covers that bush, it is time to go," said the dog. "When I get to the black ribbon, I stand to the side of the bird. Then the flash comes, and I can go to the other side."

"What do you do to come back?" asked Dad.

"No! I hadn't noticed, but they have to ask the questions," said the dog as he pointed to EJ and Manny.

"You said you didn't want them close to you!" said Dad.

"Don't act smart," said the dog. "You know the rules."

So Dad went over to EJ and pretended EJ was whispering in his ear.

"He wants to know how you can come back," said Dad.

"That's better," said the dog. "From the store I run. After I cannot see my shadow, then I head to where the bird sits, on the other side, and wait for the flash," said the dog.

Fidelio told Dad that all the signs pointed to exactly noon. Dad went back and pretended EJ whispered in his ear again. All EJ would say was "Taka, taka, taka."

"He wants to know what day you do this," said Dad.

"You guys are so dumb. It has to be when there is no second sun at night," said the dog. "You go the next day."

Fidelio had it figured out. It had to be at noon, before the new moon would come. He told Dad what he had figured and said that he was sure of it. Finally! They had a time, day, and a place where they had to be, to travel back home. They looked at the dog, and the dog was thinking about how dumb they were.

"Okay, Mr. Dog, you have put the last piece of the puzzle together, and we thank you," said Dad.

"You can meet me there," said the dog.

"Why would you do that for us?" asked Dad.

"Oh, it's not for you," said the dog. "It's for my friend that lives on the other side."

"Who is your friend?" asked Dad.

"His name on the other side is Thor. He lives in your house," said the dog. "He asked me if I had seen you on this side. So don't think I did it for you and those two little killer viruses you have with you," said the dog.

"You know Thor?" asked Zeke.

"Yes, and just so you know how dumb all of you are, you released me from your control when you answered my question and didn't even know it," said the dog.

"Well, just so you know, we knew we would release you, from the start," said Zeke. "So who is the dumbass now?"

Everyone laughed at the dog, and he just looked at them with his ears up, and his head tilted to one side. "Thank you, Mr. Dog," they all said as they walked off.

CHAPTER 19

THE GRAND ESCAPE

As they walked home, Fidelio mentioned that they didn't have much time, since there was no moon tomorrow and it had to be the next day when they would head to the road. Dad sounded excited and told Zeke, EJ, and Manny to hurry so they could tell Mom and Aly the excellent news and get everything ready. Soon they saw their house on the horizon, and they knew they would make it in time. As they walked in the house, they told everyone the excellent news, and everyone got ready for the next day.

The next day came, and everybody was up and ready to go early. They packed their stuff in the car, and Dad told everyone that if they left anything behind, they would lose it forever and they would not come back for it. Dad went to tell Ramon and Ramona to get ready, and they were ready in a minute. They would join the family in their car to the same spot where they were when the flash came.

Everyone was in the car early and ready to go. The bear came by and asked if they wanted him to take care of the rent. At this point nobody cared and told him to save it for the next one that came to the house. They ignored him and took off. Fidelio feared this contraption, as he called it, because he had never been in a car before. When they got to the road, they saw the dog sitting across the road.

"He has to go to the same point where he came here," said the dog, pointing at Fidelio. "You can't take him back to your world for he belongs in another one," said the dog.

Fidelio remembered a bush he was standing on when he came here. He remembered because the bush had a bunch of thorns. He also remembered a big white rock, where he thought he had dropped a pouch containing some of his magic charms. He thought this was the reason he could not find his way back, because all his power was in that bag. When he looked around the rock, he found it, and he regained his power back. Everyone could tell by the look on his face this was important to him. Dad told Fidelio about how much the entire family thought of him and how much they would miss him. Fidelio told them that there's no need to miss him. He remembered that before he came here, there were white people taking their pictures, and maybe they could see the pictures in their world, for their world was exactly like his. The only difference was time. With that, Fidelio went to stand at his spot, when suddenly the big flash came again.

It blinded everyone for a few minutes, but strangely, nobody was afraid this time.

As soon as they could see, Mom yelled, "Yes! We are back!"

Dad decided they were going to go back home and make sure everything was okay, since they were gone for a while. He made a U-turn, and this time the road went the way it was supposed to go. The first fast-food place they saw was with a big yellow sign. The kids cheered as Dad pulled in, and they had something they had craved for the longest time. They finally made it home, and Mom went to unlock the door, and everyone was eager to get inside. They walked in and everything was in place the way they had left it. Thor was outside wagging his tail. Aly ran over and hugged him, and she noticed he still had food in his bowl. She called her friend to thank her for feeding him all this time and got an enormous surprise.

"Natalie, thanks so much for feeding Thor. They trapped us in a place and it took forever!" said Aly.

"Wow! They trapped you for all of three days?" said Natalie.

"Three days!" exclaimed Aly.

"You okay?" asked Natalie.

"Yes," said Aly, wondering why she had said three days.

Meanwhile, Dad was unloading the car and noticed Mrs. Lerma, the local FBI rep, outside watering her lawn.

"Good afternoon," said Dad.

"Afternoon?" asked Mrs. Lerma. "It's only ten o'clock."

"Okay, sorry. Good morning," said Dad.

"Good morning," said Mrs. Lerma. "That was a brief vacation."

"Short?" asked Dad.

"Well, three days isn't much, you know," said Mrs. Lerma.

"Well, it seemed like it," said Dad. "Talk to you later."

Dad rushed inside, and when he got to the kitchen, Aly had already told Mom about her conversation with Natalie. Dad looked as if he had seen a ghost.

Mom said, "Calm down. The important thing is that we are back."

Everyone agreed, and still they wondered.

After about three weeks, everyone seemed to fall into their usual routine, Dad going back to work, Mom working on her crafts, Aly going to visit friends, Zeke back to tennis practice and camp, and EJ and Manny just seeing what trouble they could get in. After about two of months, during summer, everyone was bored of the small swimming pool at the country club. They were not sure if they wanted to go anywhere anymore. Dad said that it had been a one-time deal and could never happen again. This put everyone at ease, and the kids started saying how much they would like to go to one of the big resorts. Dad asked Mom if she was okay with taking them somewhere.

"I am not going west anymore!" said Mom.

"Me neither," said Aly.

"I want to go to a pool," said Zeke.

"Yay! Pool," said EJ and Manny.

"We'll go but it has to be in a city where we know it is not gonna happen again," said Mom.

"Okay, I am a little scared myself," said Dad. "We'll go east for a change, where there are water parks and hotels and stores."

"I couldn't agree with you more," said Mom.

They made the plan that they would travel east to a big city where there were water resorts, hotels, room service, and, according to Dad, a lot more cars to get caught if something happened.

The planned day came, and it excited everyone on this next trip, for they were sure it would be fun. They made the usual arrangements. Aly set up Natalie to feed the dog, and Dad asked Mrs. Lerma if she wouldn't mind monitoring the house. Mom cooked nothing, because this time they were headed where she knew there were plenty of places to stop and eat.

The day came for the trip, and everybody packed their stuff in the car and was ready to go. Dad got the directions on his GPS and off they went. As they were on the road, there was a storm coming from the direction that they headed. Dad announced that this was nothing compared to some storms he had driven in while on his way to work. Dad slowed down because it was getting dark with all the storm clouds coming over them. Suddenly things got dark, and Dad pulled over in a rest area and let the storm pass. After the storm passed and they could see again, as Dad turned the wipers on, *they could not see any road.*

"Oh no, not again!" everyone yelled.

ABOUT THE AUTHOR

J. Castillo was born and raised in a South Texas town known as Laredo. He is the youngest of ten children, raised in a humble home, but filled with love. His family would travel from South Texas to Minnesota, Michigan, and Wyoming as migrant workers. This was the way of life for the family year after year. He would work long hours in the ranches and fields working cattle or picking some produce.

In Minnesota, he would work in the sugar beet fields. In Michigan it was more produce, such as cherries, pears, apples, and finally cucumbers. Wyoming was more the ranch type of work, working cattle, breaking horses, and all-around ranch work. The family completed the work before winter, so they could travel back to Texas. They scheduled school around work because everyone had to work to help. His parents raised him in a traditional Mexican-American home filled with their rich culture, food, and traditions. This was where he got his work ethic. J. Castillo also worked for the fire department as a paramedic and then transitioned to the oilfield where he worked until the coronavirus.

At the urging of his wife, he took a DNA test, which confirmed the suspicions he had carried in his heart for the better part of his life. He found out he is 98 percent Native American, Chiricahua Apache! After the original tests, other tests followed, and it confirmed all. This explained why his parents could not give answers that made sense to him, for example, where they came from. When he found out about his real heritage, it all made sense to him. His grandparents had adopted the Mexican traditions and learned Spanish somewhere along the way, to avoid persecution, which came from both sides against the Apache, Mexico and the USA. His parents have both died, but he feels a strong tie to the Apache. He is trying to get registered with the Chiricahua Tribe. His lineage, according to DNA tests, is as follows:

Chief Felipe Castillo, father of Ramon Castillo
Ramon Castillo (Geronimo's shaman and who was imprisoned and died in Arizona), father of Matias Castillo
Matias Castillo, father of Jose Castillo
Jose Castillo, father of the author